JANE WITHERS
and the Swamp Wizard

An original story featuring
JANE WITHERS
famous motion picture star
as the heroine

By
KATHRYN HEISENFELT

Authorized Edition

Illustrated by
HENRY E. VALLELY

WHITMAN PUBLISHING COMPANY
Racine, Wisconsin

D1378055

CONTENTS

Cokey Greeted Jane Enthusiastically

JANE WITHERS
and the Swamp Wizard

CHAPTER ONE

COKEY'S HUNCH

"Expect a mess," Cokey said, smiling a warning. "We got here a couple of weeks later than we'd planned."

"A mess won't scare me out," Jane laughed. In the five minutes since she had alighted from the train, she must have laughed or chuckled at least five times. A smile a minute. Because she felt deeply happy, content. It was good to be with Cokey again, and her mother. Neither had changed too much. Cokey was taller, thinner. Like everybody else, she was going through the process of growing up. She would soon be, definitely, Miss Cordelia Champlin.

But, no, Jane pushed the thought aside. Cokey would keep on being Cokey. There was too much against her, against her being dignified. Her hair, for one thing. It flew about, clinging to her thin cheeks, to her chin, a mop of cornsilk. A strand, Jane remembered, had a way of getting into Cokey's mouth. There was one in her mouth now.

9

She had insisted on carrying Jane's bag, and put it down. Pulling her hair free, she motioned with a wide gesture to the sedan at the curb.

"Station wagon, family car, moving truck," she announced. The thick, dark lashes that fringed her round blue eyes came down as if to blot out the sight and Cokey sighed deeply. "It's a wreck," she said hollowly, and looked into Jane's beaming face. "Asking a lot of you, Jane, but —"

Alice Champlin laughed, the silvery sound Jane had longed so often to hear. "It gets us there," she said, and her eyes, as they rested on Jane, added, "And it's getting *you* there with us, today. And we're so glad to have you!"

Jane thought again, that one of the reasons she had always been so fond of Cokey was because of her mother. Alice Champlin never did seem old enough to have Cokey for a daughter. And now, she looked younger than ever in a reddish, plaid suit. Atop her shining, red head, she wore a bright green beret. A bow of the matching color was about her throat loosely. But the colors were right. Alice Champlin always did look right. Polished and poised. So different from Cokey.

Jane said, "You know I'd just as soon ride in a hay rack," and grinned at Cokey who was massaging her hand. "I told you to let me carry that!"

"What you got in there?" Cokey demanded inelegantly, in the direction of the bag at her feet. "It weighs a ton!"

"A present for you," Jane told her. "Some creams I discovered. I hope——"

And then Alice Champlin's laugh cut in.

"I hope, too, Jane," she said. "I never give up hoping." Her eyes, a greener blue than Cokey's, went from one girl to the other. Cokey had on a soft rose jumper over a white blouse. But there was a dark blur on one sleeve, and several inches of the skirt hung forlornly where the hem had been torn.

"I got her out of one of the apple trees just before train time," Alice Champlin said. "Look at *Jane,* my dear!"

"I am," Cokey said, and the two of them regarded her once again with frank admiration. Her dark hair fell softly to her shoulders under a brown beret, accenting her blue eyes. She wore a neat brown and green shirtwaist frock with striped tie and pocket and a narrow brown belt. The matching jacket was folded over Jane's arm.

"You look just simply marvelous, Jane!" Alice Champlin said, for the third time. "We're going to have a wonderful visit!"

Jane was aware of the flush mounting in her cheeks. She was grateful to steer the conversation away from herself. "Oh, I know I'll have fun!" she said eagerly, and her eyes went over the broad pavement that guarded the small red-brick station. She had caught a glimpse of it in that first breathless moment before she had left the train. The sedate black letters painted against the square of white. BURLEY. The village of Burley. But little could be seen of the row of buildings across the tracks, because of the thick foliage of the immense intervening trees. It was midafternoon, a perfect day in late summer. Not hot, and not stuffy.

Jane said, in a burst of happiness, "Oh, it's so clean — and so nice!"

Alice Champlin laughed ruefully. "It should be. We've had rain for one solid week."

"Today was the first letup," Cokey added, "in honor of your visit, Jane." She looked toward her mother, and the car at the curb. "Are you caught up on the thinking, Moms?"

A little frown creased Alice's forehead. "I think so," she said slowly, and gave Jane the swift explanation, "We're out, you know. Quite a way from the village. I always try to remember everything before we leave."

Cokey said, "Well?"

"I think so. Yes, I'm sure of it." Alice motioned toward Jane's bag. "Put it in front with me, Cokey. You and Jane can have the back seat and catch up a little. Two years is a long time!"

But Jane had the bag in her hands. "Just open the door," she told Cokey. "It's my turn now."

There was a little fluster as they got under way, and then the car went bouncing over the tracks, past the bending branches of the trees, and the road that was the heart of the village lay before them. First there were stores on either side, and then the houses, frame buildings, that seemed to grow out of the street itself, because they were set so closely. Some had fences at the side, white, low wooden fences, where vines trailed and flowers grew tall and bright. There were some trees, but most of the yards were at the backs of the dwellings.

"Not Main Street," Cokey pointed out. "This is Prim Street."

"It fits!" Jane said. "Oh, Cokey, don't you just love it?"

"Oh, sure." Cokey tossed her head, to get her hair back. "But we're not villagers, you know. We're farmers — or we will be."

Jane knew. She had almost memorized Cokey's letter which brought her the invitation to visit the Champlin's. One of Alice's cousins had heard of the place, and had told them. Alice had been completely won, and so had Cokey — and Eddie.

Eddie was Cokey's younger brother. Jane remembered him with a guilty start.

"Does Eddie like it as much as he expected?" she asked.

"He's wild about the place. Right now he's gone to the city to see about a tractor. He knows a man who knows a man who's got one." Cokey was sitting on the edge of the back seat, but she slid farther back. "Eddie calls the farm the 'Not So Good Earth,' but he says we'll wrest a living from it."

"Not so good—?" Jane said.

"Oh, that's Eddie. But the place *is* run down. It was empty for months. Three old ladies lived there. They didn't do much about farming, I guess. Couldn't get help."

"But you have apple trees," Jane said eagerly.

"There must be a hundred!" Cokey was leaning forward again. "Well, maybe not quite a hundred," she amended, and broke off to point to where a cross road cut over the highway. "We turn down there, to the right."

They had left the village behind and had come to the top of a hill. Spread below them was the countryside, a patchwork quilt of greens and golds and fainter touches of reds. The vivid blue feather-stitch of a river cropped out here and there.

"I can't believe it!" Jane breathed. "I'm really and truly here! Two years *is* a long time! Cokey, do you think you're going to live here—always?"

"It seems so. If Moms wants us to, of course. *She* says it's up to us. Dad is still in Washington. We won't see much of him. But then, we didn't any-way—lately. We hope he'll be coming home to stay before so very long. *He'll* love it here."

Why, Jane did not know, but the thought came to her suddenly that Cokey was not altogether sat-isfied. That something was annoying or troubling

her. Two years was a long time. But even so, Cokey
had never been jumpy—keyed up.

That, Jane decided, described Cokey now. She
was jumpy.

But why? Her letter had sounded so enthusiastic,
so eager.

Jane told herself it was her imagination.

"We had company this afternoon," Cokey rattled
on swiftly, "just before your train came in. That's
why this jumper." She spread out the skirt, noting
with no particular alarm the torn hem. "The Toudahls called on us. I wish you'd been there, Jane.
You'd have loved it. There was Grandma Toudahl,
and Mother Toudahl and Mary Lou. She's about
our age." Cokey hesitated for an instant. "I liked
her."

Jane said, "Oh" with interest.

Alice turned her head slightly to say, "We're almost there, Jane!"

The car was jouncing now over the side road, and
a thick spattering of mud flew from the tires.

"Awful, isn't it!" Cokey said. "If it rains while
you're here—" She peered out of her window. "And
my guess is that it will!"

Jane was looking ahead. "It won't matter," she
said. "What's a little rain, Cokey?"

But the puddle ahead was a treacherous looking
one. "Hold on!" Alice called out, and the girls fell
silent, while the car sank down, but came up grimly,

bringing them to a firmer road. Ahead, through the grove of apple trees, Jane saw the house.

It was brown, with white windows, a low white door. A house of no particular period, but Jane guessed that it had started out as a little square one, and as time went on, it had been enlarged. There was a kind of sedate little white porch cutting in at one side, with, a low wing jutting out from there. Among the apple trees, the brown house was the same color as the trunks of the heavily laden trees.

Jane drew in her breath on a long, ecstatic "Ohhh!"

"It is sweet, isn't it?" Cokey exclaimed. There was nothing uncertain about the way Cokey said it. A kind of sturdy defense, and pride no one could doubt.

"Oh, yes!" Jane said. "It's perfect."

"We think so, too," Alice added. They drove around the side of the house, to a door where only one stone step rose from the thick grass. Alice turned around. "But, remember, Jane, we're not really settled."

"It won't matter," Jane assured her. "I'll help you settle!"

"And that settles that!" Cokey said, opening the door. "Let's get going."

It was warmer, Jane thought, now that they were out of the car. Alice insisted that it was her turn to carry Jane's bag and proceeded to the house. Cokey muttered something about "Going to rain again," and the three of them went inside.

It was cool in the house, and the smell of fresh paint was in the air. There was a clutter of furniture in the long living room, where the walls were a gleaming white.

"Imagine the way it's going to look," Cokey said. "Sweet, don't you think?"

Alice patted Cokey's shoulder. "Take Jane to your room, Cokey." She smiled at Jane. "The bedrooms are done, thanks be, and the kitchen and dining room." She gave Cokey the bag. "Hurry now, honey. I'll rig up an—" She paused, and the smile faded abruptly on her lips. "Oh!"

"What is it, moms?" Cokey sounded alarmed.

"Eggs! I forgot the eggs!"

Cokey's sigh was audible. "Oh, I thought something terrible had happened. We'll go get some."

"But I thought an omelet—" Alice said, still dismayed.

"I'm not hungry," Jane assured her. "I mean," she grinned, "toast'll do. Or—any old thing." She took Cokey's hand, and was surprised to find that it was cold. "Come on, show me around," she said.

"This way." Cokey went ahead, down a narrow hallway. "There's no upstairs," she pointed out. "I mean, it isn't finished off, and we won't need it anyway. Our bedrooms are all in the south wing. No matter how hot it gets in the daytime, it's always cool at night."

"That's something," Jane said, but it was with an effort that she made herself hold to her original enthusiasm.

Cokey was speaking like a real estate dealer, showing a place to a prospective purchaser, but Jane had a sense of chill, as she had when she had taken Cokey's hand, and when she had felt how alarmed Cokey had been over nothing, really nothing at all.

They came to Cokey's room. It was big and there were five windows, two of which looked out, through crisp, criss-cross curtains, to the twining trunks of the apple trees. The walls were the softest green. A dressing table and a low chest were painted white with rose-colored knobs. On the twin beds were spreads with a rose design over green flounces. Two chairs and a square stool were mahogany. Jane remembered them, but the pink upholstery was fresh and new.

"We did it all ourselves," Cokey said, and tried not to let herself sound too satisfied.

But Jane was warm in her praises. "You've done wonders, Cokey. It's beautiful." She watched Cokey putting down her bag on the stool, and when the girl turned, Jane's thought must have been just so many words, for Cokey grinned suddenly with the impish gaiety Jane knew so well.

"You're wondering if it won't make a new woman

of me," Cokey said. "Coming out of a rosy room like this, I *should* be something."

"Well," Jane laughed.

"I can, honestly, if I have to," Cokey went on, "but I'm not like Moms, Jane, and I'll never be. I feel best of all in my slacks. After all, this *is* a farm. But Moms insisted on this kind of a room." She took Jane's jacket and her hat and hung them in the clothes closet. "Anyway," she said over her shoulder, "I'm glad we got a lot of beds. Oh, Jane—I hope you can stay forever!"

There it was again, that curious, urgent note, so new, so unusual in Cokey's voice.

"I'd like to," Jane said. "It's so—so quiet and beautiful here."

Her eyes were turned toward the windows, toward the gleaming red of the thickly hanging fruit. But she heard Cokey's sharp little sigh and looked at her quickly, so that she caught the shadow that seemed to darken the blue eyes.

There was a strange, small silence between them, the quiet that comes before a flood of words. Cokey had something she wanted to tell her, Jane knew. She wanted to take the thin hands that were held so stiffly clasped, the hands that were so strangely cold and say, "What is it, Cokey? What's wrong? Tell me! You know you can tell me anything!"

But she made herself wait. There was a long stretch of time between them. Cokey was the same, and yet so different. Her whole surroundings were new. Jane felt suddenly lost, uncertain. But there was a bridge that could bring them together. There were all the years they had known each other, the joys and the small sorrows they had shared.

Oh, tell me, Jane thought. Please, tell me, Cokey.

And she knew, when the girl said, "Jane—" motioning to one of the mahogany chairs, that the bridge had been crossed, that they were really together again. Jane seated herself. Cokey brought the other matching chair close. "I—I want to ask you something," she said, her eyes drifting away, but coming to dwell directly on Jane's eager face. "I—I hope you won't laugh."

"I won't," Jane promised.

"It's—"Cokey's fingers trailed over a fold of her skirt. "It's about a queer feeling you get that you've done something exactly over, the same way, when you know it couldn't be possible." Her face looked white, drawn. "You've had that feeling, haven't you?"

"Why—yes," Jane said, trying to keep her voice quiet, firm. To minimize Cokey's worry, whatever it was. "I guess everybody feels that sometime or other, Cokey."

"Do—you think I'm making mountains out of molehills?" Cokey asked.

Jane managed a small laugh. "How can I think much of anything?" she replied reasonably. "You

"I—I Want to Ask You Something," Cokey Said

haven't told me what your molehills are."

A soft puff of a breeze brushed against the white curtains. Cokey's eyes went to the windows unseeingly, and came back to Jane.

"It was this afternoon," she said, in a hushed, strained voice. "I told you the Toudahls called. That was why I had to get into these duds quick."

Cokey paused and Jane felt a desire to urge her to hurry on, to pass over the unessential details. But she said, quietly enough, and with a trace of amusement, "I'll bet they're the aristocrats of the village."

"They've lived here always," Cokey said seriously. "Moms gave them tea in the dining room, and Mary Lou and I went out to get them a basket of apples. We talked about schools and the places we'd been and so on, and she said she hoped we'd stay here always and that sort of thing. And all at once she asked me if I'd heard about Simmering Springs."

Cokey paused again, moistened her lips and went on, "I said no, I hadn't, and Mary Lou looked around as though she suspected there were eavesdroppers and—and then she said, 'Well, then, you haven't heard of the Swamp Wizard.' And I—"

"The—Swamp Wizard!" Jane repeated, bending forward, uncertain she had heard correctly.

"Yes, Swamp Wizard," Cokey said. Her eyes were on Jane's face, but not seeing her in that moment. "That was when I got the—the feeling. I thought to myself that I'd stood right here before under the apple trees. Just this exact way, with Mary Lou looking as though she'd seen a ghost and asking me about the Swamp Wizard." Her eyes met Jane's squarely. "And, of course, it had never happened before."

"Well—that's nothing to be terribly upset about, is it, Cokey? Except," she amended, "you don't hear of a Swamp Wizard every day." Jane's calm attitude was deliberate, pointed to relieve tension stored up within Cokey.

"No, you don't," Cokey said stiffly, refusing to rise to Jane's lighthearted attempt to treat the matter as unimportant. "And—that's not all, Jane. I got," she seemed to choke, "one of my hunches." Her eyes were wide with apprehension. "You remember?"

"Yes, I remember, Cokey, but—"

"When Eddie played in the basketball finals," Cokey cut in, "I said his team would win, that he'd win for them, but he'd get hurt. That's exactly what happened."

"I know—" Jane started.

"And the time Moms was going to take that plane," Cokey interrupted, "and I begged her not to. She thought I was silly, but she finally gave in and took the train. And you know how lucky she was that she listened to me. That plane was wrecked!"

"But, Cokey—" Jane made another attempt. "Just because you were right, doesn't mean such a terrible lot. I mean, I can make guesses, too."

"Sure, you can," Cokey agreed swiftly. "Anybody can guess. I'm not talking about guesswork. I'm talking about my hunches. You ought to know. I told you when you took that high ski jump that time—"

Jane laughed, but not too convincingly, for Cokey was weaving a spell about them, a mood that Jane was impatient to break. The laugh helped a little. "I would have tumbled anyhow," she said. "Almost everybody else did."

"But you didn't walk for a week," Cokey pointed out. One slender hand came up, silencing Jane's further denial. "You can say what you want to, Jane. I know when I get a hunch. I tell you, I know!"

"All right," Jane gave in. "What's your hunch now?"

"It's about—what Mary Lou told me—about the Swamp Wizard."

It was said in a tone of dire prophecy, and Jane felt the chill breath of a cold wind. But the wind that ruffled the white curtains was heavy and warm and sweet. She said, somewhat impatiently, "What about this Wizard? Who is he? Did Mary Lou tell you? You never heard of him before, did you?"

"No. But that doesn't matter. I had the hunch right away, *before* I knew."

"Before you knew what, Cokey? Don't be so mysterious."

"I can't help it. That's the way it is. Mary Lou's scared stiff of the place. Everybody in the village is. Nobody'll go near there."

"Near where?"

"Simmering Springs. Even Mary Lou's never seen the place. I guess her mother did, years ago."

"Why are they afraid?"

"Because it—it draws like a magnet." Cokey's voice sank to a whisper. "Because, if you get in there—you never get out. It's—worse than quicksand."

Silence hung between them, heavy and unbearable. Jane shook her head, pushed back her dark hair. Cokey seemed like a stranger. She wanted to bring her back again, to make her forget the wild tale she had heard.

Because that was all it could be—a wild story, village gossip. In such a small place as Burley the people must create their own excitement. There could not be much excitement on Prim Street as Jane had seen it.

Jane said suddenly, "Does Alice know about all this?"

"Moms—?" Cokey's eyes went even wider. "Heavens, no! And—this time, I don't want her to. I want to keep this away from her. I—I have a feeling that this is my battle, Jane. Somehow, this

Swamp Wizard—"

Jane had heard enough. She stood abruptly.

"All right, Cokey." One hand went to her friend's shoulder. "You're in this alone and you're going to handle it your own way. But, it seems to me, you're a lot more gullible than you used to be. You never saw this Mary Lou until today and—"

"That doesn't matter," Cokey said dully. She sighed and came slowly to her feet. "It's just one of my hunches."

"Which," Jane pointed out, "have sometimes been wrong."

"Yes, they have," Cokey said, slowly, thoughtfully. "I have been wrong—sometimes."

"And my guess," Jane went on swiftly, "is that you're wrong now. You heard something new and unusual, and you've dramatized the whole business. Honestly, Cokey, I wish you'd make up your mind to be an actress. You'd make such a good one."

"Not me." Cokey shook her head. Color was coming back into her cheeks. "You carry on for both of us." Her eyes were warm again, glowing. "Moms and I are so proud of you, Jane. You—"

"Swell," Jane cut in. "Now, suppose we get into our slacks. I didn't bring a lot of clothes because you told me not to."

"That's right." Cokey moved toward the closet again. "I have things that'll fit you." She pushed the row of hangers that held various garments to one side. "This'll make room for you, Jane. I'll help you unpack."

But before Jane could open her bag, Alice called and then appeared in the doorway.

"Well—" she looked from one to the other. "I thought you'd be all changed into your working duds long ago. I need a couple of helping hands."

"We talked," Jane said, with a grin, letting Alice believe that they had covered some of the time that had separated them.

Cokey did not want her mother to know what she believed was an evil that threatened their happiness. And it was just as well, because it was probably nothing more than idle chatter. How could anything like a Swamp Wizard harm this happy family in the brown house under the apple trees?

"I made lemonade, and rounded up some cookies," Alice said. One hand brushed her hair back from her forehead. "The air's getting heavier, girls. I think you'd better just grab a bite and then dash back to the village for the eggs. I don't want you to get caught in a rain storm."

"Neither do we!" Cokey said fervently for both of them. Her hand on Jane's arm urged her back down the hallway, past the dining room, which Jane glimpsed as a large room with a bay window, and into the kitchen. This was a spacious, divided room, with a breakfast nook filling one half. It was decorated in olive green, a deep orange and a creamy tan, and the windows were bordered with gay paintings of fruits and flowers. The board which came down from the wall to form the table in the nook, was down now, laden with a great green pitcher and an orange plate heaped with cookies.

"The planning board," Cokey explained. "We figure out here what we're going to plant and how —and we also eat here."

"Hurry up and do that now," Alice urged them. She poured the lemonade, but her eyes went to the brief green curtains at the window in the nook. "I wonder if you should go—or wait till tomorrow," she said.

"Oh, we'll be back in no time," Cokey assured her. "We'll get the eggs at Hendrick's. That's not far." She looked out at the sky. "I don't think it'll rain right away, Moms."

"Perhaps not," Alice said. "I want you here, snug in your beds if it storms."

She could not know—none of them could know —that the girls would *not* be here, safe in this happy haven when night came, when the storm would break in all its fury, and when it would seem that there might be some truth in Cokey's hunch.

CHAPTER TWO

ONLY SEVEN MILES

Cokey had gone ahead, out the back door, but Jane hesitated a moment, went back and made a pretense of snatching another cookie from the plate, to Alice's pleased amusement. But she did want them to hurry. Jane shouted, munching the cookie as she rushed out, "We'll be back in no time. These cookies are so good!"

"I'll make another batch tomorrow," Alice promised.

There was not time to really look about, but Jane caught a glimpse of several large buildings set back from the house as the girls hurried around to the side where the car was standing.

"I hope it's light enough for you to show me around," Jane said breathlessly as they got inside. "I mean when we get back."

"I think it will be," Cokey said, but not too convincingly. "If it doesn't rain." She backed the car several yards, turned and they were again headed toward the muddy side road.

They passed the deep rut, and the going was easier. "I do like rain, really," Cokey put in. "I mean, we can talk, and there's plenty to do in the house. Only, of course, it takes the paint so long to dry."

"Is there a lot more to do?" Jane asked.

"Painting? Oh, scads. Mom means to give the place a complete going over." Cokey gestured with her head toward her window. "Look over that way, Jane. Did you ever see land that sort of—sort of—"

"Lumped like that," Jane supplied the words, "but so soft, you wanted to pet it."

Cokey laughed. "Jane, you're precious. I think it—but it takes you to say it!"

A little quiet settled between them as they looked out, a pleasant quiet. Jane had to stop once as a boy with a dog drove a herd of cows across the road.

"Always stop for a cow," Cokey said. "I wish we had some. If our plans go through, we will. Chickens and pigs, too. Mom's got such wonderful dreams. I hope they come true."

"Why not?" Jane asked reasonably. They were proceeding, and it seemed Cokey had turned onto a new road, one which they had not traveled on the way out. Jane looked at her, but Cokey's face was turned so that only the line of her cheek showed. It looked thin and tight.

She's thinking about that wild story again, Jane guessed, as she recalled the strange, tight-lipped girl who had confided in her in the dainty rose room. What a new and different Cokey—a girl caught in the mood of terror. Well, Jane thought, she'll forget it. We'll be so busy having fun, she won't think of it again.

But what was it Cokey had said? The whole village was afraid to venture near Simmering Springs? It drew like a magnet once you got in—! Jane drew herself together abruptly, sitting up more erect. She looked again toward Cokey, who was bending down a little, looking upward toward the sky.

"Will we make it?" Jane asked.

"We'll miss the worst of it," Cokey murmured.

But Jane was thinking of the girl who had visited at the Champlin home, Mary Lou Toudahl. What sort of a person was Mary Lou? After all, Cokey had only the girl's story to go on, and maybe Mary Lou was a good story teller. But Cokey had liked her.

Jane looked down at her own hands and found them clasped tightly together. She wondered if she was letting herself believe in Cokey's latest hunch. She shook back her dark hair. I won't believe it, she told herself firmly. I came here to have fun, and fun it will be!

They had come to a scattering of houses. Jane heard the bus behind them. Cokey slowed down a little and the immense, blue machine shot by.

"That's the—" Cokey began, but the words were lost, cut off, in a sharp cry of alarm. Or perhaps it was Jane, herself, who had cried out, for certainly, she saw the thing happening in the same instant.

To the right of the road was a clump of tall lilac bushes. From behind them, a woman had come, rushing toward the road. She had fallen, almost directly in their way.

The brakes screamed as the car came to a jolting stop. Cokey's voice was high with terror. "Jane— Oh, Jane! Did I—?"

"It's all right," Jane heard herself saying. "I think we stopped in time, Cokey." Her hands were opening the door. She was out on the road. "It's all right," she reassured Cokey. "Come on, let's help her. I think she's hurt."

The woman — a tall, thin figure with white hair—was lying on her side, moaning. Her hands were gripping her right ankle. Her hat had come off and her hair had loosened over one faded cheek. Several feet away was a small, black handbag, long and narrow.

With several quick movements, Jane snatched up the bag, the hat, and she and Cokey helped the woman to her feet.

"Can you stand up?" Jane asked her. "We didn't hit you, did we?"

"No," the woman said breathlessly. "No, I'm sure y' didn't." Her voice sank to a sob. "I missed it! After the way I hurried all day—I missed it."

She must have been in a great hurry, Jane thought, by the way she had dashed out without looking to see if the road was clear. Well, she had much to be thankful for—her injuries could have been serious.

"And my ankle," the woman quavered. "To top it all, I—"

The girls were helping her toward the path behind the lilacs. A square cottage nestled in among tall elms and thick clusters of shrubbery. As they walked toward the little house, the woman kept up her woeful repetition, but she seemed much more concerned over having missed the bus, than injuring her ankle. Jane guessed that the pain must be intense.

When they reached a low, screened porch, Jane whispered to Cokey, "You better find a doctor. I'll take her in and make her comfortable."

"Can you manage?"

"Oh, sure."

The woman gasped, "You won't need—t' go far. Doctor Albins — next — house. Tell him — Mrs. Burke."

"All right," Cokey snapped, and to Jane, "I'll hurry!"

But first she pushed open the door, so that Jane could assist the woman inside. Then Cokey flew out again, and Jane was left with the injured woman.

They came directly into a small, low living room which was completely filled with three chairs and a couch. A window massed with various house plants let in a muted light. If Jane had not heard the chirping of birds, and the sudden spurt of song, she might not have noticed the two cages. As she helped the woman to the sofa, she said, "There now, you'll feel better. It sounds as though your canaries are glad to have you back so soon."

The woman would not be comforted. "I shouldn't be here now," she moaned. "I should be on my way. I shouldn't be here!"

"Maybe you can go tomorrow," Jane offered. She was on her knees, removing the low, stub-toed oxfords. "Perhaps the doctor can fix you up in a hurry."

But the ankle was badly swollen already and it looked serious. Even as she said the words, Jane knew that Mrs. Burke would not be able to walk on it for some time.

Mrs. Burke knew it, too.

"He won't let me go," she said, her head twisting against a red plush sofa cushion. She put her hands behind her, forcing herself to a sitting position. "Just let it be," she said. "There's nothin' more t' do, till he gets here." From the depths of her heart she gave a heavy sigh. "That's th' way it goes," she said. "You plan an' plan—and everything goes wrong." She seemed to become aware of Jane, standing at her side, and she said suddenly, "You're a good girl to help me. You're both good girls."

"Oh, we were glad to help you," Jane said in a rush. "I wish there was something more I could do

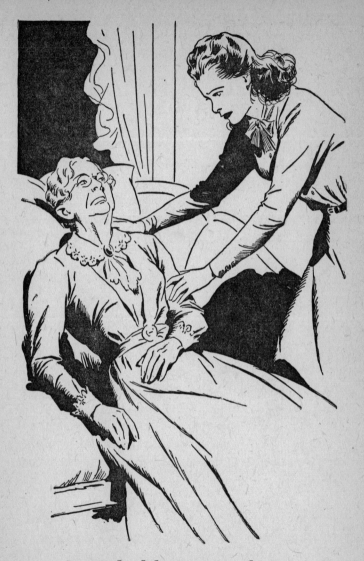

Jane Helped the Woman to the Sofa

to make you comfortable."

"No." The woman sat straighter, one hand pressing down upon the knee above her hurt foot. "No. There's nothin' to do—now. But I did want t' go so bad. I've been so worried. It's so long since I've had any news — all of two weeks."

"Were you going far?" Jane asked, not out of curiosity, but the woman seemed to want to tell her troubles.

"No, not far. Only seven miles." Her voice choked again. "And I went and missed that bus!"

Jane murmured her sympathy, and Mrs. Burke seemed to gather strength to continue. "It's my sister. Mrs. Bill Keegan. She lives over in the hollow." She paused, looked at Jane thoughtfully. "You're new," she said.

Jane nodded. She wished the woman would relax, and that Cokey would come with the doctor.

"And that girl," Mrs. Burke motioned with her head, "she just come here, didn't she? Seems I saw her in at Hendrick's once, and somebody said they bought the old Benton place."

Jane did not know whether or not Cokey's home had once been the Benton place, so she said quickly, "Yes, the Champlin's are new here. And I'm visiting them. We were on our way now to get some eggs," she added without knowing why.

A spasm of pain flickered over Mrs. Burke's face.

"Please," Jane said, "let me take care of that

ankle. I know something about first aid."

"Mebbe," the woman said, and paused an instant. "But y' don't know Doctor Albins. No. Just let it be, please. There's somethin' else I want you t' do. Somethin' much more important." Her eyes were imploring. "If y' only would!"

"Why, certainly," Jane said. She came closer to the couch and dropped on one knee at the woman's side. "What is it, Mrs. Burke?"

The woman took another deep breath. "Get your eggs at my sister's place. It's only seven miles down the Baker Road. Y' can't miss it. The first house on the right of the first side road, after you hit the Baker road. Then you can tell her—what happened. But tell her I'm all right, y' understand? I just want t' know how they all are. It's been raining so much. I'm worried. I want to know how they all are."

It had taken a tremendous effort, but the woman did not give in to the pain, nor take her eyes from Jane's face. "Would y' do that?" she asked.

"Well—it's not my car," Jane said. "I'd like to, as far as I'm concerned." She met the pale eyes, and felt her throat thicken. "Oh, I'm sure we can!" she said impulsively. "I'll tell Cokey—I'll explain. I'm sure she'll do it."

The woman leaned back, a pitiful picture of relief. Now I've let myself in for something, Jane thought, and Cokey is in such a hurry to get back! And Alice is waiting. Oh, whatever made me go and make such a promise?

She heard the footsteps of Cokey coming with the doctor.

She said quickly to Mrs. Burke, "I'll explain things, and I'll let you know right away."

"Thank you, my dear," the woman murmured. Her eyes were closed, and her face seemed to tense against the pain. But Jane heard her murmur, "Bless you!"

While the doctor tended the hurt ankle, Jane and Cokey stood on the porch, and Jane unburdened herself. Cokey listened attentively until Jane had finished. It did not take long.

Cokey said, thoughtfully, reluctantly, "Well—"

"Oh, I know I had no right to tell her we'd go," Jane cut in. "It was—well, she was suffering so. I spoke before I really thought. I'll go back and tell her we simply can't make it!"

They both heard the murmur of pain that came from behind the closed door of the living room.

"We've got to go," Cokey decided on the instant. "The poor thing! It isn't far. I wish there was some way we could tell Moms, but we haven't a phone at the farm." She stood for a moment, biting her lips. "But Moms would want me to, I know." She gave Jane a little shove. "Go in and tell her. We've got to get going."

Jane knocked on the door, and heard Mrs. Burke's "Come in!"

"We'll go," Jane told her swiftly. "But we might not get back here tonight. Would it be all right if we stopped in here tomorrow?"

"Oh, that'd be wonderful!" the woman said. The doctor was bending over the couch, and Jane caught only a fleeting glance of her face. But it was enough to assure her that she and Cokey were doing a work of mercy.

Jane called, "Don't worry, now. I'm sure your sister is all right. We'll see you tomorrow." And she left, closing the door softly.

Cokey had parked the car at the side of the road, near the lilac bushes. The girls were silent as they hurried to it. Hands on the wheel, Cokey turned to Jane. "The Baker Road, you said. Did she tell you which direction that was?"

"No, and I didn't think to ask." Jane felt the impact of what she had done, and again a guilty pang. "Maybe we could—" she began, but Cokey's hand was on her arm, silencing her, as she called out to a man across the way, "Can you tell us how to find the Baker Road?"

The man stopped and looked at them as Cokey repeated the question. The space between them was not wide. Jane saw the strangely puzzled expression on the man's face. He said, slowly, "Why, yes. You go straight ahead, past two forks in the main highway. Take the third fork to the right. That's the Baker Road." He had come nearer to them, and before the girls could thank him for the information, he asked "You plan t' go way down into the hollow?"

"I don't think so," Cokey said. Jane knew she was eager to be off. The air was much heavier—and so was Jane's heart. Instead of helping Cokey to hurry back to Alice and the brown house under the apple trees, she had caused her to head in the opposite direction—into the oncoming storm. A weight pressed upon her spirits, but something more, something she could not name. What was this nagging worry that eluded her? She heard Cokey thanking the man, saw him blotted from their sight as the big sedan rolled down the road.

"I feel so guilty," Jane began.

"Don't," Cokey corrected. "We'll make it, Jane. We've got to make it."

Jane lapsed into an unpleasant silence. As the car headed on, a thought pounded out its dire warning: "You shouldn't be here. You shouldn't be doing this. You should make Cokey turn back."

Jane fought the dark mood. After all, it was only seven miles. They had passed one of the forks. There was one more, then the turn onto Baker Road. The sky was threatening, and it was growing steadily darker. What was so dreadful about a summer rain?

The answer to that question came before many moments. They were traveling steadily downward, and on either side of the road were deep ditches filled with muddy water. The sight did not brighten Jane's spirits. A summer rain, she reflected, could be a cloudburst.

"Anyway," she heard her own voice cutting into the quiet with a forced gaiety, "anyway, we can get the eggs at the Keegan place, Cokey. And I did tell her we'd be back to see her tomorrow morning. That should save time."

"Poor thing. There wasn't anything else we could do, Jane!" Cokey said, trying to reassure herself, too, that they had little choice but to go on, even though she knew it might not be the thing to do.

Cokey motioned with one hand to the ditches. "That'll give you some idea, Jane. When it rains here, it pours!"

"Oh, I hope it waits for us," Jane said fervently, aware that they were passing the second fork in the road. "We'll soon be there, Cokey."

But when they came to the slender sign that read "Baker Road," and took the turn as they had been directed, the mailbox that leaned out at the roadside bore no name like Keegan. It was a longer and entirely dissimilar name—Hagstrom. The girls read it and exchanged quick glances of alarmed surprise.

"This is it," Cokey insisted. "This has to be it— but it isn't."

"No, it isn't," Jane had to agree. "But I'm sure she said the first house to the right." They looked up a steep hill, criss-crossed with deep cuts where other vehicles had made valiant ascents to the house at the crest. Jane acted quickly.

"You wait here," opening the car door, "I'll walk up and ask them."

"But—your shoes!" Cokey tried to protest.

"It'll be easier on these mocs than your tires. At least, I won't have to keep to the road. I'll cut up here, through the grass."

And before Cokey could offer any objection, Jane was gone.

She had not progressed far when two lean dogs, white, with spots of brown, came rushing toward her, barking lustily. They were not unfriendly, and as she went on toward the house, Jane assured them she was a friend. The dogs seemed to understand, and followed her to a flight of wooden steps which led up to the farmhouse kitchen.

A woman stood in the doorway. At a word from her, the yelping dogs quieted, and Jane asked, "Would you please tell me how to get to the Keegan place? We're trying to find Mrs. Bill Keegan."

The woman, tall and big-boned and pretty in a mild, placid way, came down the steps. "The Keegan place?" she repeated. "You going there, now?"

"Yes. Is it far?" Jane did not like the way she was looking at her, the concern in her face.

"Well, no," the woman said. "But some of the road's under water, and the bridge is—" She paused and glanced down the hill. "But, you didn't come in a truck?" she asked.

"No, we have a car," Jane replied, and after a few moments of silence she repeated, with a shade of impatience, "Which way is it, please? We have to hurry. We're trying to beat the storm."

The woman looked at the sky. "It's going to pour," she said. She had come all the way down the steps by now and was standing beside Jane, one hand pointed downward, to the right, in the direction the sedan was now headed.

"You go straight ahead, till you come to the bridge. You can see the river from here."

Jane saw it. A dull gray form that seemed to have no banks. Trees on either side of it appeared to grow out of the water.

"Well," the woman continued, "cross the bridge. Take the turn to the right, and it's the first house." She sighed and shook her head. "Not much of a place. I been meaning to get over there." She caught herself quickly, afraid that she might have hurt the girl's feelings. "You a relation?" she asked.

"No," Jane told her. "Just bringing her a message from the village." She moved away. "Thank you ever so much."

"You're welcome," the woman said. And after Jane had gone some little distance, she called out, "I'd go as fast as I could."

"We will!" Jane called back, and with all possible haste returned to Cokey. Again they were on their way. Jane tried to tell herself that she had been imagining things again—that the darkening sky and the heavy air caused her depressed feeling. But she knew, in her heart, that there was something in the woman's attitude that had brought to life the fleeting, nameless worry that had dogged her thoughts before. Nothing unusual had been said, but an undercurrent of fear and danger marked the harmless words. The woman had been surprised to learn that they were going to the Keegan place. No, not exactly surprised, it went deeper than that.

"Well, here's the bridge," Cokey said, suddenly.

Jane gave a start. She had not seen the low, flimsy bridge from the rise of ground, or she might have wondered that it rated the name. It seemed to touch the water that flowed beneath it. No wonder she asked me if we were driving a truck, Jane thought.

But the structure appeared sound enough and they drove over it without mishap.

"Whew! I'm glad that's over," Cokey said, fervently, "but now it's starting to rain."

Thick drops slapped against the windshield, and from far overhead came the roll of thunder.

Jane moaned, "Oh, Cokey!" less because she was afraid of a storm, than because she felt that this had been her doing.

"We'll make it," Cokey insisted. "Gosh, it's getting dark!"

As though it were a derisive contradiction, light-

ning flashed, brilliantly sharp. The thunder that
followed closely was a deafening clap. Cokey stopped
the car.

"I forget," she said, "do we drive on in a storm,
or do we wait? Is it safer in a car, or under a tree?"

"I think the best thing would be to try to make
the Keegan place," Jane responded. "According to
Mrs. Burke, we should have been there long ago.
But then, she was in such pain. I suppose she got
mixed up." That was in the past, and Jane knew it,
but it was something to say—something to cover up
the flash in her mind that had come as sharply and
as swiftly as the lightning. She had the fleeting
worry now. It had taken definite form. Only seven
miles, Mrs. Burke had said. It should be a simple
enough matter to find someone else to go to her
sister's for her, someone from the village. Because
Mrs. Burke must know everybody there. She had
begged the girls to go, begged a stranger! *Why did
she have to ask a stranger?*

Jane did not want to answer that question, because she might answer it correctly. Because—
"Let's go on, Cokey," she said. "Let's get to the
Keegans'." There was light enough to see the road
ahead, as it turned and lost itself in and among the
low, twisting oak trees. "It's not far now, it can't be."

"Okay," Cokey said as she started the car, "but
don't look so gloomy, Jane."

"Gloomy?"

"Well, guilty, then, or filled with remorse. I could have said no."

"But—your mother, Cokey. She'll be worried."

"Oh, Moms knows I'd have sense enough to get out of a storm."

That was true enough. So, perhaps, she would not be too upset. The storm would delay them, but it might not last long. They could wait at the Keegans' till the worst was over, then they could go home.

But could they?

Cokey heard it, too. The great thundering sound, and the rush of water that came in one of the deathly quiet interludes between the thunder claps. Jane said, "Oh, Cokey—the bridge!"

And then Cokey leaned back, twisting away from the wheel. Her icy hands gripped Jane's. She clung to Jane, sobbing, "Oh, Jane, I'm so frightened! I can't drive any more. Oh, Jane, please, will you?"

"Of course, I will. Don't be frightened, Cokey."

"B-But—we'll never get back now. Never!"

Another flash of lighting—another thunderous peal. Jane held Cokey tightly, murmuring reassurance. "There must be another road. There's sure to be one. Soon as the storm lets up, we can start back. There's nothing to worry about."

Now the tables had been turned. Jane had seemed to lose her own fears. They were blotted away, absorbed in Cokey's wild terror. Rising to the need to comfort the girl, Jane, herself, grew stronger, surer.

"Slide over," she said, pushing Cokey behind her, while she squirmed under the wheel, "I'll get us over to the Keegans' in a hurry."

"Oh, what would I ever do without you, Jane?" Cokey said.

Jane managed an almost convincing laugh. "You wouldn't get yourself into a mess like this."

"Oh, don't say that. I knew all along we shouldn't have gone—but I wanted to help her, too."

So, Cokey knew, too, they should not have gone. Perhaps she, too, had thought of the strangeness of Mrs. Burke's request. Perhaps she wondered, also, why Mrs. Burke could not find someone in the village to call on her sister.

But it did them no good to look back and bemoan their kind impulse, Jane thought. The thing to do was get to the Keegans', purchase the eggs, and return home. This seemed right and sensible.

Despite the flashes of white lightning and the thunderous blasts, despite the gush of rain that seemed like a blanket of water upright before them, barring their way, Jane felt that they should go on. As the rain became heavier, the thunder and lightning abated.

Cokey kept her two hands about Jane's right elbow, not too tightly to impede her driving, and certainly in no way causing her to miss their way. Yet that is exactly what happened. They had missed their way.

The road between the twisted oaks had continued its erratic winding. They had crossed a small culvert, and then come to the high, square house that loomed whitely before them. To the left was another building with one side fallen in decay. The glare of the headlights revealed for an instant the tangled metal of unused machinery, and then shone squarely on a screen door which opened, it seemed, to the kitchen of the large farmhouse.

"All right," Jane said, switching off the ignition, "let's make a run for it."

Cokey hesitated for a moment. "All right," she said faintly, and opened her door.

As they bent their heads and ran, it seemed to Jane that she heard the faraway barking of a dog, though none appeared to challenge their arrival. She arrived first at the screen door and knocked. Light from a window poured out into the wetness, evidence that the house had occupants, but minutes passed and the wooden door remained closed.

Jane knocked again and put her hand to the brown knob. Suddenly it turned and the door seemed to open by itself. As the girls rushed in out of the storm they almost collided with a woman whose outstretched hand was reaching for the knob.

To their surprise they were not in a kitchen, but in an outer shed, and the light was none too good. Backgrounded by the glow that came from the open kitchen door, Jane could see a woman, who stood there gasping in astonishment, and advancing no welcome whatsoever. She was a thin, square-shouldered woman, and Jane had the strange sensation that she was going to ask them to leave at once.

But, thought Jane, when she knew they were sent by Mrs. Burke, she would feel differently. Jane, of course, presumed that the woman before her was Mrs. Keegan.

Jane found her voice. "We're sorry to rush in here like this, Mrs. Keegan, but we were getting soaked."

The woman turned slightly, so that the light from inside touched her face, and revealed her dark hair, parted in the middle, and smoothed tightly to her head. Her thin, long features were characterized by high cheekbones and deep-set black eyes which regarded them blankly. "Mrs. Keegan?" she said in a deep, toneless voice. "I'm not Mrs. Keegan."

"Not—Mrs. Keegan?" Cokey echoed. "Then who—?"

"I'm Mrs. Frieson. This is the Frieson place."

The girls looked at her blankly, unable to comprehend their error, or the woman's fiercely aloof attitude. As though to force her explanation home to them, the woman added, "This is Simmering Springs. It's been the home of the Friesons for ninety years."

The home of the Friesons—Simmering Springs! The place—of the Wizard of the Swamp!

CHAPTER THREE

LIKE NOTHING HUMAN

The gaunt mistress of Simmering Springs must have sensed the girls' dismay. She could not help but be aware of the manner in which they shrank back and away from her. If she were regarding them as unwelcome guests, it must have been obvious to Mrs. Frieson that their wish was to be away from the house—miles and miles away.

Perhaps this realization caused Mrs. Frieson to soften, to make a grudging inquiry of their unexpected arrival. She looked from one taut face to the other, asking both of them, "Do you know the Keegans?"

Cokey shook her head wordlessly, but Jane found her voice. It sounded far away in her own ears.

"No. We—we don't know them," she uttered. "We were coming to bring them a message."

"A message?" the woman repeated.

"Yes. From Mrs. Burke. She—she was coming herself today, but she hurt her ankle. She asked us to come for her."

Mrs. Frieson gave a low, derisive grunt. Jane thought at first that her word was being doubted. Her dark head lifted. "It's the truth, whether or not

50

you believe it. Mrs. Burke was worried about her sister."

"She should be," the woman said, looking away from them, so that the light from the kitchen door fell over her face again and highlighted her thin and set mouth. "The Keegans are flooded out," she continued emotionlessly. "They're moved in with the Millers, probably. I wouldn't know. We don't mingle." Her eyes came back to rest on the girls. "You could tell *that* much to Martha Burke, though. Her sister's place is under water."

She must dislike Mrs. Burke fearfully, Jane thought. If we had to come to the wrong place, why in the world did we have to come here?

But it went much deeper than that. It was unfortunate to be at the home of a woman who was not a friend, but this was Simmering Springs as well! This was the place which the whole village of Burley held to be a place of fear and dread. The place which was destined in Cokey's hunch to bring sorrow and misfortune upon them all.

And they were here, now!

Cokey's hand on Jane's arm was pulling them farther away, toward the door. Jane looked quickly into her wide and pleading blue eyes.

Yes, they must go. There must be a road, another road, beside the one through the twisting oaks. It was still raining heavily. The beating of the drops came with a merciless rat-a-tat-tat upon the tin roof.

Jane patted the hand on her arm and tried to control her voice. "We're sorry," she said, "to have troubled you. We'd like to get back as quickly as we can, but the bridge is out."

"It is?" Alarm cut through the woman's tone. "You mean the big bridge, not the culvert leading in here?"

"Yes, the big bridge."

Jane thought of the ugly, gray water lapping up against the trees. It had full sway now, ripping the boards, tossing them along. The bridge had never been anything wonderful, but it had been an escape to safety on higher, firmer ground. Now, there was only the swollen river. She felt Cokey shivering, and patted her hand again. "Mrs. Frieson," she said, "is there any other way we could get back to the village?"

The woman stared at them intently before she answered. Then she said, slowly, "No, there's no other way."

"But—but—!" Cokey protested.

"But," Jane gasped, "there must be another road. There has to be! How will we get back?"

"I don't know how you'll get back," the woman said in a tone that seemed almost malicious. "The road to the east has been under water for almost a week. We haven't been able to get through to the city ourselves."

Jane's heart was pounding in her throat. Her

"We'd Like to Go Back But the Bridge Is Out."

mind was raging against the situation into which they had been unwillingly drawn, and she caught the impact of that word, "city." Mrs. Frieson had said they had been unable to get to the *city*, not to the village.

But what difference did it make, Jane tried to philosophize, fighting through the mists of fear that hung so heavily about her—the fear that they were to be forced to remain in the inhospitable house of the mistress of Simmering Springs.

"What are we going to do, Jane?" Cokey almost wept. "We've got to get back! Mom'll be so worried!"

"Stop crying!" Mrs. Frieson rebuked harshly. "That never did anybody any good." Her eyes pierced Cokey, who cringed closer to Jane but closed her lips against another sound. "There's nothing else you can do but stay here," the woman grunted. "I can't turn you out in this storm."

"Oh, you wouldn't want us to stay," Jane protested. "It would be too much trouble. We couldn't—"

"No, I don't want you to stay," the woman interrupted to admit. "I don't hold with the village, and the village don't hold with me." Again the thin mouth twisted. "But I haven't been called a *witch*, not yet anyhow." She moved abruptly to the kitchen door, opened it and went inside. "Come in," she told them.

Jane heard Cokey's trembling breath, and tightened her grip on the girl's hand as they moved slowly, reluctantly, into the kitchen. Mrs. Frieson went ahead, toward a wood stove which, by contrast with the shabby outside appearance of the home was a thing of clean black iron and gleaming chrome. She lifted one of the lids and pushed in a chunk of wood.

Jane thought she heard the woman mutter: "Girls! I never thought a girl—"

The rattle of the iron lid drowned out the rest, and Jane closed the door behind them. They both stood, looking about the long, low room, feeling the balm of the warmth that came from the stove. They were in a combination kitchen and dining room. A round table was at the far end of the room, near another door. On a wall shelf above it was a wooden clock, which gave the time as eight-thirty. Near the clock was a narrow window with a wide sill, which held pots of flowers. More flowers and plants were perched on two other windows along the outer wall. Between these two windows was a cupboard which rose almost to the ceiling. It had glass windows, through which could be seen white, gold-rimmed dishes and a single dark blue cup with a large handle. On the opposite wall of the room were curved-hook hangers, set in a row the full length of the room, on which were hung a ragged buff sweater and a blue coat. Underneath the hooks was a couch, higher at one end and covered with a patchwork quilt, which obviously served as someone's bed.

Jane saw at a glance the strange contrasts present in the room in which she stood. It was neat and, with only a little effort from the woman, it could have been inviting, whereas Mrs. Frieson was anything but warm and agreeable. She did not for a moment let the girls forget that they had been forced upon her—that they were two uninvited and unwelcome guests.

From the light of a lamp on a bracket near one of the center windows came a better picture of Mrs. Frieson. She was older than Jane had at first thought. Deep-cut lines ran from her nose down to her mouth, and there was a touch of white in her smooth, black hair. She wore a green dress of heavy cotton with its sleeves pushed up on her arms. Her hands, holding the edge of her pale-green apron, were short-fingered and square—the kind of hands which might be called capable of hard work.

The word teased Jane. Yes, Mrs. Frieson was capable—capable of making them feel miserable. She seemed to be studying them, and Jane had the distinct feeling that she might at the instant be regretting the invitation she had extended.

Jane and Cokey stood before her, sensing her apparent displeasure. There was not a sound in the room except the metallic ticking of the clock. Outside, the rain dashed against the windows.

Finally the woman seemed to come to a decision.

"You might as well wash up," she said, motioning with a jerk of her head to the wall where the girls were standing. "I'll get you some supper."

Jane saw the wash basin resting in the hollow of the white sink close beside them. Three towels were hanging near it on a triple bracket. One of the towels was long and of a sturdy-appearing fabric, but the others were smaller and whiter.

"Take one of the little towels," Mrs. Frieson directed.

Jane hesitated only an instant, then took the handle of the small pump at the right of the sink and filled the basin. Cokey, close beside her, whispered, "Oh, Jane, it couldn't be any worse!"

Jane did not know why, but she answered softly, "Maybe it could. We'll make the best of it."

Painfully the two girls rested on stiff chairs near the table and watched the woman place dishes before them in hostile silence. Then came her gruff command to eat and hurry along to bed. Although Jane scarcely knew what it was they had eaten, she tried once to say that the supper was delicious and to thank the woman, but her effort to express her gratitude went unheard or unnoticed. From her chair near the stove Mrs. Frieson waited for them to finish and shifted her eyes alternately from the clock to the back door.

She's waiting for Mr. Frieson to come in, Jane thought. Maybe she wants us out of the way before

he arrives. Perhaps when he appears it will be all
the worse.

The apparel on the hooks told her little of the
kind of person Mr. Frieson might be. She only
knew if he were anything at all like the mistress of
Simmering Springs, it would be well for them to
be out of sight when he arrived.

Cokey made the same valiant effort to eat, but
the food choked her. Jane caught her eye, and read
the words lips did not need to speak—let's tell her
we're finished and get away from here, where we
can talk things over.

As they left the table together, Cokey made an
attempt this time to thank the woman, but her little
speech, too, was ineffective. Mrs. Frieson came hur-
riedly toward them, and from the lower shelf of the
cupboard she took a squat lamp. As she lighted it,
Jane said:

"Could we help you with the dishes?"

The woman turned to her. "No," she snapped,
"there's nothing you can do." With this reproof she
struck a match and soon had the lamp burning.
"Now, you can follow me," she ordered and led the
way past an archway partially hidden with a heavy
blue curtain. This led to a door, which opened to a
flight of steep, narrow stairs. "We sleep downstairs,"
the woman stated, "but you'll find the bed upstairs is clean."

Jane felt as though she had been slapped. "Why

—I'm sure it is, Mrs. Frieson. Your—your whole house is so nice and clean. We're—very grateful to you."

Lamp in hand, the woman paused for a moment and looked the girl so squarely in the face that Jane felt her cheeks flame. It seemed that some of the icy reserve in the woman had melted, and she was about to say something bordering on politeness.

"How do you know?" Mrs. Frieson said in a tone that completely fooled Jane. "You haven't seen my whole house. There's plenty that say it isn't fit to live in!" And with this she started on up the stairs.

Jane patted Cokey reassuringly on the shoulder and grasped her icy fingers as they slowly climbed the narrow stairs.

Mrs. Frieson paused at the top of the stairs, where a railing ran down a hallway. There were closed doors, one to the right, the other to the left, but she motioned ahead.

"You'll have the room back here," she told them. "Don't lean too hard on that rail. It needs to be fixed."

They followed her with reluctant steps down the hall, to the lone door. Mrs. Frieson opened it, went in, and set down the lamp. She came out again, immediately. "This is where you'll sleep," she said.

Jane glanced into the room and back again to the woman's face. Mrs. Frieson did not seem to expect any word from either of them, and it was probably as well. In that moment, Jane could think of nothing to say. The woman gave a short, weary sigh, turned and went on down the steps. She did not ask them to leave their door open until she could see her way to the stairway, but the door was left open, and the girls stood, rooted before it. They heard her going down, step by step, and then the closing of the door below.

"This is where you'll sleep," was what she said, and when Jane looked again into the room, the words re-echoed in her ears. She felt restless, like some sort of a mechanical puppet that had been wound up too tightly. It was like watching herself in a dream, and she half expected to find herself awaken and find that it wasn't real. She heard the door close and Cokey's half-subdued sob startled her into reality. She put her arms around the girl's thin shoulders.

"It's like a prison," Cokey whimpered. "A horrible prison. I'm s-so frightened!"

"Shush," Jane told her gently, and rose once more in courage. She looked about the room. "It's not such a bad prison, Cokey, and the bed really looks comfortable."

"Comfortable!" Cokey moaned. "There's not an inch of comfort in this place. I never saw such a— such a stone woman in all my life!"

It was so apt that Jane could not suppress a chuckle. It was a weak shadow of a laugh, but it served to lighten the situation for both of them. Cokey drew away.

"Well, isn't she?" Cokey demanded.

"Completely frozen, if you ask me," Jane said definitely. Cokey put one fist up to push away the moisture in her eyes and to brush back her blond mane. "Oh, Jane," she said despairingly, "what are we going to do?"

"I don't know—yet," Jane admitted. "We'll have to hold a conference." She looked back at the brass bed, encouragingly high and smooth under its white, thick spread. She sat on the edge of it, drawing Cokey to her side. "Let's talk it over," she suggested.

"I don't know what I'd do without you," Cokey sighed.

Jane gave a rueful laugh, and replied, "We went over that before." Her eyes were moving about the room. The lamp was shining serenely from a heavy, oaken chest of drawers. There was no mirror over the chest—only a picture of a blindfolded woman seated on a globe, bending over a kind of a harp. Under it was the single word *Hope*. Near the chest was a window, its dark green shade drawn. Besides the chest there was a low washstand with a white pitcher and a white bowl. Nearby was a rocking chair with a cracked leather back and seat. Above another chair, stiff and straight backed, hung a picture of a woman in a filmy red dress and a huge red hat. In her hand she held a red parasol. The picture was bright enough but the woman's great, green eyes and the inexpressible sadness of the face were out of key. It stared straight at Jane, and she looked away.

"We've got to keep on hoping," she said.

"For what?" Cokey asked bluntly. "Here we are, locked in this awful house. And not only that, Jane, we're *here*—at Simmering Springs!" Her eyes were wide, accusing. "You wouldn't believe me when I told you about my hunch. But you see—I was right!" Her voice had sunk to a hoarse whisper. "Maybe you'll believe about the—the Swamp Wizard now."

Jane's fingers closed quickly over Cokey's knee. "Listen!" she said. "I think someone's down there —talking to Mrs. Frieson."

"But, what—?"

"Just listen, Cokey. We've got to find out all we can!"

They sat in strained silence. Jane's finger went to her lips, warning Cokey against the slightest sound. She got off the bed and tiptoed cautiously to the door. Very quietly she opened it and peered out into the hall.

A man was talking to Mrs. Frieson. Jane turned and motioned to Cokey, who tiptoed to her side and they both stood listening tensely.

The girls guessed that the man must be standing

at the foot of the stairs, for snatches of his words came up to them. Jane distinctly heard, "Downright dangerous—," a low mutter and then, "Must be out of your head!"

"He sounds like an *old* man," Jane whispered in Cokey's ear. "Let's go over to the top of the stairs. Maybe we can hear more."

"But—Jane—!"

"They won't hear us, and they can't see us because we'll keep back. If the door does open down there, we can sneak back to our room." She had Cokey's hand and was moving cautiously along the hall, drawing the girl with her.

Mrs. Frieson was saying something, too low for them to hear, but when they reached the head of the steps, the man's voice came again, and Jane could see why. The door below had not closed tightly. A long crack of light showed through the darkness.

"You know what's goin' to happen now, Alma! It's goin' to come again, like it come every time before!" He was an old man, a greatly upset old man. Alma must be Mrs. Frieson's name. Somehow, it did not seem to fit her. Alma had a cozy, happy sound.

Jane strained forward again to listen. Mrs. Frieson's words were inaudible, but the old voice carried.

"I heard them in here. Mabbe it was all right t'

feed them, but they shouldn't be here this long, Alma. It's goin' t' come. The Swamp Wizard—!"

Cokey gave a gasp that just missed being a cry of anguish, and Jane whispered frantically, "Don't you dare, Cokey! Don't you make a sound!"

"Oh, Jane!"

"Listen!" warned Jane, afraid that Cokey might have been heard; but Mrs. Frieson's voice raised at the moment so that neither she nor the old man could have caught the sound.

"Don't say that," Mrs. Frieson commanded fiercely. "There is no such thing! There never was!"

"Oh, you're stubborn, Alma," was the reply, and Jane could imagine a head shaking.

"You always was stubborn. Never would admit the truth."

"You've no right to say such a thing to me, father!"

"I don't mean one day an' another. I mean—about the Swamp—"

"Father, will you please go back to bed!"

The old man might be looking at her pityingly, or he might have moved away, for Mrs. Frieson went on talking, too low for the girls to hear.

"Perhaps she's warning him that we're likely to hear," Jane whispered. "Anyway, Cokey, you can tell that *she* doesn't believe the story about the Swamp Wizard—whatever that is!"

"I'm not so sure about that," Cokey's voice came

in a tense murmur. "I think she doesn't want to believe in it!"

"Oh, Cokey." Jane was about to say that Cokey was hopeless, when they heard the old man talking again.

"When's Lem comin' in? Is he still out in the barn?"

Mrs. Frieson's reply could not be heard.

"Why don't he get rid of that critter?" the old man fretted. "She's always ailin'. I wish th' boy was in here. It ain't safe out tonight."

"Father, will you please go back to bed? You'll be sick tomorrow."

The old man laughed harshly. "I can't feel much worse than I do right now! Waitin' for it t' come." The girls heard him stamping about. "Why don't Lem come on in! He must've seen their car! He ought t' know by now what t' expect!"

Mrs. Frieson apparently tried to console him, to urge him more gently to return to his room, but the old man flatly refused.

"I can't sleep, I tell you!" he said shrilly. "If Lem'd only listen t' me, he'd a got rid of that cow. He'd be in here now, safe." His voice changed, took on a note of cunning. "Or maybe th' Wizard'll take care of *her,* like he did Rosette."

"Father!" Fear and exasperation mingled in the cry. It was clear that Mrs. Frieson was being goaded almost beyond endurance.

"All right, all right. But you wouldn't go out there, would you? *You* wouldn't go an' bring Lem in?"

There was a pause, an interlude so still, it seemed the lower floor of the house had been suddenly emptied. Jane and Cokey, standing at the head of the stairs, their hands tightly clasped, could not know the underlying cause of the conflict between father and daughter. They had understood only half of what had been said, but this much was evident: Both stood in deadly fear of the thing, or the person, that was called the Swamp Wizard. The old man had admitted its existence, and the woman had refused to do so, but both were in the grip of an unearthly terror.

Jane heard Cokey choke, heard her weak little murmuring voice, but Jane's fingers warned the girl to be still, to wait. Would Alma Frieson accept her father's challenge? Would she go out to bring in the boy who was called Lem?

Mrs. Frieson's voice cut abruptly through the heavy stillness. "I'm going. I'll show you, once and for all—"

"Y' won't go, daughter! I won't let y' go!"

"You can't stop me, father. After all, he's *my* boy."

"But—Rosette. Y' remember what happened to Rosette!" The old man's voice had undergone a change. He was pleading, brokenly. "You were only

"You Can't Stop Me, Father," Mrs. Frieson Said

a little thing, then. Not more'n five years old. But Rosette was yours. I give her t' you—"

"Father, *please* go to your room. Wait there. I'll be back soon."

"Put down that coat, Alma. Put it down, I say!"

"I have to get him, father!"

There came the sound of quick footsteps. A door slammed. There was a moment of quiet, and another door shut. That would be the outer door, the door that led from the shed. Alma had gone out into the storm, to get Lem, her boy.

But the old man seemed to hope that she might change her mind, that she might listen to him, and come back. His cry, "Alma! Daughter! There'll be two of you!" was a piteous thing, doubly so, for it must have fallen only upon the heavy air. There was no answer.

He must have moved about, because the girls could hear footsteps above his pathetic whimpering. Eventually he came back to the foot of the stairs, back to the door that did not close tightly.

"There'll be the two of them!" his voice quavered. "It'll come, like it always does. And th' two of them —out there!"

Jane was not aware that both of Cokey's arms were about her, almost crushing her, until she heard the girl gasp, "Oh, Jane! What is it? What's going to happen?"

Jane's throat was dry. Staring down at that long

slice of light, she felt hypnotized, unable to move, even to take her eyes away. She whispered, "I—don't know, Cokey. We'll have to wait."

Not for long. The thing that the old man had fearfully prophesied must be the sound that broke the silence in the next moment. It was a cry, a screeching, unearthly cry, that seemed to come from the outdoors.

"Did you hear that, Cokey?"

"Did I hear it!" Cokey's panic-stricken fingers bit into Jane's arm. "Oh, Jane, what *was* it?"

"I don't know. But it was like nothing human!"

"The Swamp Wizard!" Cokey's whisper came from lips that might have been frozen.

And from below, the words were repeated with frantic flaming fear. The old man cried out: "I told 'em! The Swamp Wizard! The Indians knew. They warned my people. But Lem paid no heed—an' now—Alma! It's come! Now—it's come!"

CHAPTER FOUR

THE INDIANS' WARNING

Jane felt the girl close beside her go suddenly limp, and tried to hold her, but she slipped down to the floor, safely away from the stairs, for which Jane was frantically thankful. Having Cokey collapse was a new worry but it somewhat minimized the horror that had gripped her upon hearing the animal-like screech and the old man's terrified jabbering. If Cokey were to give in this easily. . . . Well, she must not permit her to.

The door of their room down the hall was open enough to show the white oval that was Cokey's face. The dark lashes were smudges over her closed eyes, and despite Jane's urgent pleading, they remained closed.

"You've got to wake up, Cokey!" Jane pleaded, trying to lift her to a sitting position. "Cokey, please wake up! I can't leave you here. And I can't carry you down the hall. He'd hear us, don't you understand!"

"Who'd hear us?" Cokey murmured brokenly. "Oh—Jane! It's you, isn't it, Jane?"

Jane's lips were close to Cokey's ear. "Cokey—listen," she whispered. "Don't you lift your voice, you understand? Remember, we're upstairs here, right at the top of the stairs. You're all right now. So get up." Her arms were boosting the girl. "Come on—get up!"

"I'm—getting up," Cokey said pettishly, and then she was fully awake, wildly aware of the thing they had heard. Her voice thickened with fear. "He said it was the Swamp Wizard, Jane. He—he said now something would happen to—both of them!"

Jane battled with her own fear. "I know, but— he could be wrong. Come on, Cokey, let's go back to our room."

They were standing now. Cokey reached out with one hand to grip the railing that ran along the hall, bordering the stairs. Jane remembered Mrs. Frieson's warning and said: "Don't, Cokey. It's not safe."

She could feel the girl trembling. Despite the pressure of Jane's hands, Cokey drew away, and her voice rose alarmingly. "What *is* safe here, anyway? I can't go back to that room, Jane. I can't!"

"Oh, Cokey—please be quiet!"

"I can't go back!" Cokey buried her face in her hands. She began to sob brokenly.

Jane's thoughts searched wildly. But there was only one other alternative. "Well, then, we'll have to go downstairs. But—I don't like to. Mrs. Frieson wanted us out of the way. When she comes back—"

"*If* she comes back," Cokey corrected dismally. "Her father doesn't think she will—he ought to know!"

Yes, Jane thought, he ought to know, but there was such a difference of opinion between the father and daughter. Or was there? Cokey believed that the old man voiced his fears, but that Mrs. Frieson only refused to admit hers. She was every bit as terrified as he was. Certainly, she had not seemed to relish the thought of going out after her son. She went because it was her duty. Yes, of course, she was afraid, and who wouldn't be? That horrible screeching cry! Jane shuddered.

Cokey was tugging at her arm.

"Come on, let's go down. The old man's all alone now. He won't bite our heads off!"

Wouldn't he? Jane recalled that he had told Alma Frieson that she had no right to let them stay in the house, and furthermore that the evil happenings that were inevitable had been *their* doing. The whole thing was fantastic, unbelievable. Such a little while ago, she, Jane Withers, had come, bursting with joyous enthusiasm, to visit old friends in the peaceful brown house under the apple trees.

Jane's thought lingered there, upon Alice, Cokey's mother, who must be suffering torment. It's all my fault, she told herself bitterly. I brought us here!

Admitting it was one thing, but there was much

more to do than that. It was up to her, now, to get them out again and, above all, nothing must happen to Cokey. The girl was Jane's own age, but she had always seemed younger. It had always been Jane who had made the decisions, Jane who had led in all the activities of their little group.

But this was no game. This was different!

There was Cokey's hand again, tugging at her. "Are you coming, Jane?"

"Just a minute." A minute to decide what was the best thing to do. Cokey's impulse was to flee from the room at the end of the hall which seemed to her like a prison. But, if they went down, their position might become still graver. They might rush right into new and fresh danger.

Jane forced herself to ask: What danger? An old man, a frightened old man? He was waiting down there for his daughter to come back. Waiting for —Jane found that there was no way to reason the thing out. It was wholly without reason. It was, and she felt the feeling return, a miserable dream. There was nothing to do but to take each moment as it would come, to keep her head as clear as she could, and above all, to protect Cokey.

"Come on," Cokey pleaded. "I'll be so glad to get down there, where there's some—some people anyhow. Don't let go my hand, Jane."

"I won't," Jane promised firmly. "Wait, now, let me go ahead."

Cokey stood still, and let Jane go before her. "Can you see the light down there?" Jane whispered.

"S-Sure, I see it. The door's not shut tight."

"I mean, enough to—" but Jane halted because she thought she had heard a door close.

"What's the matter?" Cokey gasped.

After a brief moment, Jane said softly, "Nothing. I thought I heard someone coming in, but I guess not. Maybe it was the old man going outdoors."

"He wouldn't!" Cokey said, with a shudder that shook even Jane.

Jane's fingers held Cokey's hand tighter. Step by step, they went on down, until they reached the door before them. For an instant they paused, listening for a sound beyond the door, but there was none. Gently, Jane moved forward. The light grew before them, almost blindingly after their time in the darkness. They were facing the far door of the kitchen, the one which had remained closed, and which, Jane guessed, led on to a porch. Ahead, too, was the clock, but Jane did not look at it. Her gaze went, as did Cokey's, to the table nearby. A man was sitting there, an old man. His hands were up over his face. He did not know they had come in.

This must be Mrs. Frieson's father. Jane wanted to say something, anything, but she seemed powerless to break the spell cast by the pathetically bowed figure. In that moment, she experienced more of

pity than of fear. The long, silvery hair that strag-
gled down over a wrinkled suede collar, the brown
vest that seemed sizes too big—that was all they
could see of the man. That, and the wrinkled hands
that seemed to be trying to blot out the room.

They must have made some sound, for suddenly
he lifted his head and turned and faced them.

There was a sharp, startled pause during which
the two girls stood, staring at the old man. His
black eyes, deeply sunk beneath silvery brows—
eyes that were bulging with fright—stared back.
He was old and his face was like parchment, folded
and creased. Furrows ran from the sides of his high,
pointed nose, and continued from his chin to his
throat.

Jane moistened her lips and tried to say: "Please
forgive us." Then the light of fear left the black
old eyes, replaced by anger and indignation. The
silver head came up higher and the old man, with
surprising strength, leaped to his feet. He was a
slight figure, not much taller than the girls, but in
that moment he seemed to tower above them.

"So—it's you!" he cried, and thrust the chair on
which he had been sitting out of his path. "You're
the cause of all this! It's all your doin'!" A knotted
forefinger came up to point accusingly. "Why did
y' have t' come here? Answer me that!"

"We—we didn't mean to come here," Jane stut-
tered. "That's the truth. It was a mistake."

"A mistake!" The man's voice rose shrilly. "Is that what y' call it? I'd say it was a misfortune!" Jane stepped forward a little, so that she might thrust Cokey behind her.

"Please," she begged, "won't you believe me? We wanted to go—"

"Then why didn't y'?"

"The bridge was washed away. We couldn't get through. And your—Mrs. Frieson said the road to the city was under water."

The old eyes moved toward the blue curtain which closed off the adjoining room near him. Jane observed that the side of his hawklike face appeared to be carved out of stone. His voice, when he spoke, was equally as hard.

"She shouldn't 've stopped y'! That's where y' should've gone." He turned a baleful face toward them. "That road goes by th' Swamp. Then *you* could've been took—*you,* instead of—them!"

He was something of a hypnotist and Jane felt the power of an evil spell, until it seemed she had been called away, rescued, by the sob that came chokingly from Cokey's lips. Jane turned to Cokey, who had one hand up to her head. She was deathly pale and seemed at the point of collapse.

"You've got to sit down, Cokey." Jane's arms were about her again. "Come over here to the table."

Cokey shook her head and drew away. She seemed unable to walk in front of the old man. But Jane

held firm. All her resolution to protect Cokey returned in double strength, and the anger that began
to seethe in her heart renewed her strength. Unwillingly, they had come to this place. Through no
fault of their own. And, whatever had happened
here, or might happen, could not, and would not
be held against them.

Cokey must have felt some of that glow. She
looked once, questioningly, at Jane, then with a
stifled sob, permitted herself to be led to one of the
chairs. This was so placed that Cokey's back was
toward the door through which they had come.

The old man had watched them with no show of
sympathy. His set lips only held back a flow of re-
proach, but when Jane faced him again, he had
little chance to speak. The girl confronted him,
blazingly.

"I don't know what's going on here, but whatever it is, it's not our fault. We wish we were anywhere but in your house right now. We wanted to
go, but were told we couldn't. If you could please
understand that, it—it might make things easier for
all of us!"

The old man was startled for a moment, but not
swept from his path.

"Make things easier!" A kind of groan came from
his throat. "Y' don't know what you're talkin'
about!" He glanced fearfully past her, toward the
back door that led to the shed. Jane waited with

him, listened with him for footsteps, but there was only the sound of rain.

"Y' don't know what you're talkin' about," the old man repeated.

"All right." Jane gathered strength again. "I don't know what I'm talking about. How can I? I was never here before." She seemed to stand back and reason with herself that she was talking to an old man in his own house. "I'd like to ask you, please," she said, with a small show of deference, "just what you meant by wishing we had taken the road by the Swamp."

"I meant that then th' Swamp Wizard would've taken you—instead of them!"

"Oh, Jane!" was Cokey's strangled cry.

Jane put a hand on her shoulder. "It's all right, Cokey. I'm going to find out—once and for all." She straightened to meet the glaring black eyes.

"What do you mean—the Swamp Wizard?" Jane demanded, again addressing the old man. Her hands seemed to clench at her sides, but she went on. "Who is he? Have you seen such a thing—or person?"

The old man's jaw was trembling. His eyes went again toward the blue curtain. "I've seen enough t' believe," he said. "Yes, I've seen enough."

This was no answer and he knew it, but he was going to tell them more, much more, Jane felt, so she waited while one gnarled hand went to rub against the sharp line of the jaw. It was as though the old man were fighting for courage now, the power to talk about some secret fear with strangers.

But first he looked toward that back door which remained so tightly closed. Alma and her boy had not come in and the old man feared to go out to them. Perhaps, to bring them closer, his story rambled and went back farther than was necessary. But Jane and Cokey were held from the start with a kind of uncanny fascination.

"You don't know about th' Springs?" his voice began abruptly, "I know—th' Indians knew. Long before our time, th' Indians knew about Simmering Springs. They called it Th' Mystery Pool of the Great Spirit. I lived near here ever since I was a boy, an' th' Springs was always th' same, always simmerin' and seethin' an' boilin'." He paused, but only long enough to take a deep breath. "An' th' Swamp is right off from th' Springs. Some of it drains down th' stream, but some sinks underground and comes up in the hollow." The lines in his face smoothed a little. "It's not bad country, only that section of th' Swamp land. It's only— bad for strangers y' see? That was what th' Indians warned. No strange foot was t' be set near Simmering Springs!"

Jane heard herself say, weakly, "I see but—didn't *anybody* ever come here—before we did?"

"Y' don't believe me!" The white head nodded heavily. "You're not th' only one wouldn't listen!

Yes—some others did come b'sides you. Plenty come. Th' Swamp Wizard waited. He give 'em a chance. Then—he took Rosette."

Jane and Cokey had heard that name before.

"Who—who was that?" Jane asked.

"Rosette?" The old eyes went past them. "I'll come t' that," he said. "That was after I come here with Alma." He was less aware of them now, talking more to himself than to them. "My wife died when Alma was a baby. Rof Frieson was my friend. An' he never was strong. Mrs. Frieson wanted t' care for Alma, and Rof needed a hand. So we moved in here. It was th' only home she ever knew. She grew up with th' Friesons' boy an' we was all happy when they got married. But Alma always seemed more like a Frieson. She was headstrong like Mrs. Frieson. You'd think they was her real parents, Mrs. Frieson anyway."

It was, really, little more than a jumbled family history, and had small bearing upon the questions Jane longed to have answered. She felt her attention waver, and turned to look down at Cokey. Color had come back into the girl's face. She frowned, a bit quizzically, up at Jane who shrugged ever so slightly.

But the old man caught it, or their mood of disinterest, for he burst out, "Y' want t' know about Rosette? Well, I'll tell y'. Rosette was a colt, prettiest little thing y' ever saw. I give her t' Alma when

"The Swamp Wizard! Then—He Took Rosette."

she was only five years old—but she remembers it, all right. Rose was th' mare's name, an' th' older Mrs. Frieson called th' colt, Rosette, as a kind of a joke. But there was nothin' t' joke about at that time Th' Springs was bubblin' up. It was a warning! We all told her not t' open that spot for a picnic place, but she wouldn't listen. She went ahead and invited folks in. She said she wouldn' have Alma growin' up alone an' afraid of people." Something like a sob choked the old man's voice. "An' that's just what happened. *That's just what happened.*"

"You mean," Jane was surprised to hear herself speaking, "she grew up alone—? You mean, Alma?"

"Yes, I mean Alma. Not right away. Th' worst happened afterward. But first, it was Rosette. Th' night all the folks had gone from th' big picnic. Rosette was took that night. There was her hoof marks near th' Springs. An' Rose'd stand near there for days afterwards. Th'—" his voice sank lower, "th' Swamp Wizard took Rosette."

There was nothing funny about it, but Jane had a wild desire to laugh. She kept her tongue still, however, and moved closer to the nearest chair. "I think I'll sit by you, Cokey," she said. It sounded feeble, silly.

"I should think so," Cokey said, sensibly for a change. "I've been trying to tell you that for the last five minutes."

It felt good to sit down in the straight-back chair.

The old man followed Jane's lead. He returned to where he had been when they had come in, but it was not so much to relax. Rather, he seemed possessed with the wish to be nearer, so that he could command the respect his story merited.

"Y' want t' hear th' rest?" he said, and it was practically a challenge. "I'll tell y'. Old Mr. Frieson died, an' Mrs. Frieson. Alma grew up an' married their boy. He was Rof, too. An' Alma was th' stubborn one. She wouldn't listen t' me, either. I tried t' tell her that a time'd come when she'd be mighty sorry. And—then, it did come. Worse than Rosette. Worse than that!"

One of his hands was on the table, gripping the edge. He was looking past them toward the door.

Cokey spoke in the thick quiet, "You mean—that —cry came?"

"Th'—cry?" He seemed to become aware of Cokey. "No. No, it didn't come that very same night, but it come soon after. Alma learned she had to keep folks away from th' Springs. An' they kept away, too. I warned 'em, and then they listened. If anyone'd come—there'd be th' cry. Th' Swamp Wizard, warning them!"

Jane exploded, "But who is the Swamp Wizard? Don't you know?"

He looked at her with a kind of horror. "No, I can't say I know. Any more than th' Indians knew. But when it's a quiet night, an' you hear th' Springs

simmerin', you believe he's there, all right. An'
when someone's been took——"

When some *one* had been taken! Taken how? And
where?

But there was no time to know the answer then,
because a commotion sounded out beyond the kitchen, in the shed. There were muffled voices and
the stamping sound of feet.

Jane came to her feet, moving instinctively between Cokey and the back door. She heard the
scraping of the old man's chair as he thrust it aside,
and sensed rather than saw him get to his feet. He
called out sharply. "Alma! Alma, is that you?"

From behind the kitchen door, the woman answered, "We're coming, father."

"They're all right," the old man said hoarsely
under his breath, as though he had to make an effort to convince himself of the truth. "They're both
—all right!" And then he was moving across the
floor, calling out to them, "Alma—oh—thanks be!
And Lem!"

The door had opened, and the two were coming
in—Mrs. Frieson and Lem, her boy. Cokey had
risen and was standing close to Jane so that Jane
heard her small gasp. Perhaps it might be astonishment because Jane's first reaction was that. Lem
was a full-grown man, tall, and powerfully built,
with wide, sloping shoulders. As he entered, he was
removing his coat. Small rivers ran from it to the

floor.

"Give that to me," Mrs. Frieson said, taking the sodden garment, and as Lem turned toward her, Jane saw his face clearly. He looked like his mother, except that his hair was wavy and thicker. His features were thin, with sharp cheekbones like hers, but there was something about his head which seemed too small on the great shoulders. His chin sloped more than Mrs. Frieson's.

The old man was fussing over him, asking him if he had got wet, which was foolish, though Lem answered respectfully enough. "I'm soaked. This is a real storm, Rob."

"Give me your hat, boy," the old man said, and practically took it. He whacked the wetness from it, so that drops flicked as far as the stove, and sputtered on the hot lids.

Mrs. Frieson had tossed off her sweater—now a heap on one of the chairs—paying much more heed to her son's coat, which she hung carefully on the rocker near the stove. It came to Jane that the three of them had not once looked directly toward the table. It seemed they were sparring for time, postponing the moment when they must acknowledge the girls' presence.

Jane thought Lem had almost lifted an eye in their direction, a swift, furtive glance but she could not be sure. It was like all the man's movements, stealthy and evasive. He was like a man under a sentence, and Jane guessed what it could be—a stalking fear—the same mysterious fear that gripped the old man—Rob, Lem had called him.

So he must believe in the Swamp Wizard, too!

Of course he did, Jane amended her thought swiftly. They all did. It was in everything they did and said. Lem Frieson's voice was hushed and rough when he said to his mother, "It's all right. It'll dry."

He was speaking of his coat, and it was obvious that they were paying so much attention to the coat because they did not want to talk to the girls.

They want us to go back upstairs, Jane thought, and Cokey must have had the same feeling because she was tugging at Jane's arm. Jane glanced at her quickly, said without words, "No, not yet. Let's wait." They stood there watching the Friesons. It could not have been for more than a few minutes, but the time stretched out, strained with things unsaid, with hateful, secret fears, until the old man broke the spell.

"I—I was mighty worried about y', my boy. When I heard—"

"Lem's here now," Mrs. Frieson cut in, "so everything's all right, father. We can go to bed."

She means us, too, Jane told herself. It was barely ten steps to the door at the foot of the stairs, but it seemed miles away—an impossible exit to make casually. But for the time being, the girls were brushed aside. The old man was not content to be put

off until some of the evening's happenings were
unfolded. He followed Lem over to the stove. The
younger man stood with his back to the girls, but
Old Rob's face, hawklike and eager, they could
plainly see.

"Where were y', Lem? In th' barn, when it
come?"

"Lem was in th' machine shed," Mrs. Frieson
snapped and, as though to silence the old man, to
drown out his voice, she began an unnecessarily
loud clattering at the stove. She was putting coffee
in a gray enamel coffee pot that must have been
filled already with water. "Lem has some sense,
father," she said over the noise. "He waited in th'
shed for the worst t' pass over."

Old Rob glanced out the window. "I thought y'
would be took, Lem," his voice wavered, and Jane
guessed he was looking away so that tears might not
show in his eyes. Lem's hand came up to the droop-
ing shoulder.

"I'm all right, Rob. There's nothing to worry
you."

"Lem wouldn't be taken!" Mrs. Frieson said
sharply. "Even—even if there were any truth in
what you believe, father. None of *us* have any need
to fear!"

That was coming too close for comfort. Jane
wished now that she and Cokey had bolted abruptly
for the stairs, but the distance to them had seemed

too great. She felt Cokey's hand reaching for hers, and took it. The old man was muttering, still looking out the window.

"None of us, eh?" he said. "Y' can say that Alma, after what happened? Y' know better!"

"I know it's way past your bed time," Mrs· Frieson said. "And Lem's cold and hungry. Let me get him something to eat—please. You've been fed, and so should he be." And, as sudden as the storm, the woman whirled to face Jane and Cokey. "And so have you been fed. Why don't you go upstairs—and stay there?"

"Why—of course we will," Jane said dazedly. "We just came down because—we heard that terrible cry and—"

"It won't come again. Not tonight." The woman seemed positive. "But bright and early tomorrow —you'd better leave."

Jane saw the three faces. The old man was still at the window. Lem had moved over toward the sink near the door. Three pairs of eyes that had shied away from them before were turned fully upon them now, a barrage of accusation.

"We'll leave as soon—as soon as we can," Jane said. "We didn't want to come here in the first place."

"You know," Cokey added bravely, "that we didn't want to come here, don't you?"

"I told 'em. I told 'em about how Rosette was

taken," Old Rob chimed in. "I told 'em what th' Indians warned us. No strange foot should be set on th' Springs!"

"Father—" Mrs. Frieson shrieked.

"Mrs. Frieson," Jane broke in, "do you believe that about the Swamp Wizard? Do you believe there is such a thing?"

The woman's lips moved but before she could speak, Lem Frieson, his jaws working strangely, moved a step forward from the sink. He had a towel in his hands, and without looking he pushed it back of him, over the basin. He looked almost as limp as the crushed linen, but his voice was harsh. "You go to bed," he said. "Don't you worry my mother any more."

"And tomorrow," old Rob jerked a finger toward the back door, "you *git!*"

"We'll be only too glad to go!" Jane said fervently and turned to the girl at her side. "Come on, Cokey."

They moved together toward the stairs. The three at the far end of the room maintained a silence that spoke volumes. Jane could feel their eyes, fearful, full of a violent dislike. She whispered to Cokey, "We'll leave this door open, so we can see our way up," and then they were mounting the stairs once more. It seemed to Jane that they were moving slowly, relentlessly, into the face of darkness and disaster.

CHAPTER FIVE

WITHOUT HOPE

"Is that better?" Jane asked, bending over Cokey and tucking the red knitted shawl about her. "There's some more stuff in the closet."

"This is—grand," Cokey replied, huddled in the rocker. "But what about you? Aren't you cold, too?"

Jane admitted that she was, but it was a dreary, hopeless chill which would require more than a coat or a sweater to relieve. She forced herself to cling fast to her resolution to shield Cokey—to keep up her spirits.

"If this is the good old summer time in this part of the country," Jane finally said, "I'll take springtime in the Alps!" What she hoped might be a light laugh came from her lips and she moved back to the closet, searching over the garments that hung there. She found a short, brown jacket, and slipped it over her shoulders.

"I guess it's because of the rain," Cokey said in a tight little voice. "But I heard that it gets awfully cold here sometimes in August and September. I— I really don't know." Cokey was just talking to conceal her trembling lips, but Jane was not misled. She saw the girl's blue eyes dart about the room, as

90

though she were seeking some avenue of escape—
an escape she knew would be impossible. "I—we
haven't lived here very long, you know. This is
something pretty new." Her eyes were wider, and
she leaped from the chair, unable to endure the
restraint any longer. "Oh, Jane, I've never been
any place like this before! Such horrible, horrible
people—and this hateful old house! What are we
going to do?"

Jane held her hands again—her icy cold fingers.
"First of all," she said, "we're going to try to get
warm. Don't lose that shawl." She tucked it in
closer about Cokey.

Her own heart seemed shrunken within her, a
thin slice of ice, but she must not let Cokey know
that. Cokey was close to hysteria. Jane went over to
the brass bed. "Come on, sit here," she said, patting
a place beside her on the white spread. "Two heads
are better than one."

Cokey hesitated for the fraction of a moment,
shrugged and came to Jane's side. The lamp on the
chest was higher now, and its rays made the smudges
deeper under Cokey's eyes—eyes which seemed
afraid to meet Jane's, and went wandering toward
the window. The green shade was still down. Back
of it there came no longer the slapping of the rain.
Jane gave a sigh, "Well, anyhow, it's stopped
raining."

"Yes," Cokey said dully, head averted. "It's

stopped raining." Her head turned swiftly, almost
angrily. "What's the good of playing Pollyanna,
Jane? You know we're in a mess. Why don't we just
admit it? Why do you keep on trying to cheer
me up?"

"Cheer you up?" Jane repeated. "Well—why
not?"

"*Why?* What's the use?" Color had come into her
face, but it drained as quickly. "You know how I
feel, Jane? I feel as though we'll never get out of
here—never!" She pointed to the picture over the
chest. In the light of the lamp, the blindfolded figure
seemed to sway on the globe. "You see that thing?"
Cokey demanded. "It's called *Hope*. But the way it
looks to me is *Hopeless*. And that's us—*Hopeless!*"
Her hands came up, covering her face.

Jane tried desperately to say something, but she
was aware of the same leaden drag upon her spirits.
They were without hope—caught up in a madden-
ingly strange drama that would last—not only this
night—many nights. Perhaps . . . but Jane could
not let the thought take hold. Face the thing, she
commanded herself, as she felt her nails digging into
the palms of her hands. Don't try to put Cokey off
by speaking silly, meaningless words of cheer. Figure it out—that's the only way.

"All right," Jane said bluntly. "If you can stop
crying long enough to give the matter a little
thought."

That did it. Cokey's hands came away from her face. She flared, "I'm not crying—I'm—I'm thinking."

"So am I. And here's what I get. We're in a mess. This whole place is a mess. It seems there's a Swamp Wizard around here that screams when strangers set foot on the place. Everyone in the family is terrified, and they—"

Cokey gasped, "Oh!"

"Well?"

"It's nothing. Go on, Jane."

Jane had to bite her lip first, but she went on grimly. "The family doesn't welcome strangers. That's the way we rate. We came in here and the —Swamp Wizard gave his screech." It was all she could do to keep her voice level. She hoped she succeeded. "Mrs. Frieson is sure it won't happen again—not tonight."

"Do you think she's right, Jane?" Cokey asked breathlessly.

"Why shouldn't she be? She's lived here almost all her life. She ought to know."

"But—suppose it *does*, what then?"

What then? What if that high, piercing screech should tear through the darkness that shrouded the Springs and the Swamp?

Jane heard herself saying, "A screech can't hurt us, Cokey. It won't be *here*. It'll be out there— away from the house."

They thought about that for a moment, the strange cry, that would come from beyond the house. Now the swamp was still, and the house, too. The rain had stopped. Downstairs the three made no sound.

"I wonder if they've gone to bed," Cokey said suddenly. A corner of the shawl came loose and she pulled it closer, over her huddled arms. "I don't hear them, do you?"

"No, I don't. They must be asleep."

Cokey drew a shuddering breath. "Oh, how *can* they?"

"Maybe they're used to it," Jane said ruefully, even while she knew that none of the Friesons nor the old man could possibly become accustomed to anything so weird. She added, evenly, "No—it's because they're sure it won't happen again, Cokey. They feel safe now. And—and we should, too."

"Snug as two little bugs in a rug," Cokey said, but she meant, miserable as two girls in a prison! She came to her feet abruptly, tossed back the mop of cornsilk hair as though the weight were unendurable. Jane watched her soberly as she went to the door and turned the knob. Their eyes met and held as Jane joined her at the door.

"Isn't there some way we could get out of here, Jane?" Cokey said in a taut whisper.

"I've been thinking about it," Jane said over the wild thumping of her heart. She had tried to think

"Isn't There Some Way We Can Get out of Here?"

it over, but it had been to no avail. Always she had come back to this forlorn upstairs room. There might be vines on this side of the house, or a tree that grew close enough—. She was certain that the porch jutted out below them, but there was only one window to the room, and when Jane had first gone to the closet to find the scarf for Cokey, she had made a dismal discovery—the window had been nailed down. At least a nail ran through the bottom of the sash. Jane had given the window a trial shove, and it had not budged.

"The window's out, isn't it?" Cokey said suddenly. "I saw you trying to open it. I wasn't that far gone! Do you think I'm absolutely helpless?"

"Oh, Cokey!"

"I'm sorry. Don't pay any attention. I—I'm thinking of Moms."

To this Jane had nothing to say. Now that the rain had stopped, she knew that Alice Champlin would be frantic with worry. There was no telephone in the brown house under the apple trees, and unless Eddie should have come home from the village, she was alone. But how would Eddie get home? The car was here, out in front of the Friesons'!

Merely for the relief of movement, Jane moved to the window, and lifted the green shade. There was the nail, its flat head a stubborn glint of silver. "I wonder," she said, "what time it is. I didn't wear my watch."

"Ten, maybe," Cokey said drearily. "I guess it doesn't matter—much."

But it did matter. They both knew how much it mattered. How minute upon minute was adding to the fear in Alice Champlin's heart.

"And there's no way for her to find out where we are," Jane said abruptly. There was a scratchy collar on the jacket she had put on, and she found the garment suddenly too uncomfortable. She slipped out of it, tossed it over the back of the rocker. "And it's all my fault!"

"What do you mean, all your fault?"

"I told Mrs. Burke we'd stop by tomorrow. I was thinking of saving time, so we could hurry back to your house tonight. Oh, if I'd only said tonight, that we'd come back to Mrs. Burke's tonight!"

Cokey frowned. "I don't exactly get it."

"Oh, you do! Don't you see, Cokey, Mrs. Burke isn't expecting us tonight. So she can't believe any-thing—anything unusual has happened."

"You mean, she wouldn't get in touch with Moms till tomorrow."

"That's it. We won't be missed till tomorrow—by the only person who knows where we went!"

Cokey shook her head. "There's no use blaming yourself for *that*, Jane. Because how could Mrs. Burke know we were *here!*"

That was true enough. How could she know they had come to the Friesons'—to Simmering Springs

—by mistake?

But there was someone who might know, or might guess—the woman who lived at the farm on the top of the hill, the woman who had directed them to the bridge. When she found out that the bridge had been washed out, surely she would set up a search for them.

Or would she?

She might think the girls had taken the other road that passed east of the Friesons', to the city. In all probability, she did not know that the road was under water, or where they were, for that matter. Even if she did know where they were, would she send anyone after them? Jane recalled the tense manner of the woman, the things she had left unsaid.

Like everybody else, *she* was afraid to venture near the Swamp!

"And, even if Mrs. Burke did know," Cokey's voice cut through the clamor of Jane's thoughts, "who could she send? Who'd come *here?*"

Jane's fingers went through her hair, back over her forehead. It still felt damp from the rain. She picked up the jacket again and threw it over her shoulders, scarcely aware of what she did.

"You wouldn't believe me, Jane," Cokey continued. "You laughed when I told you I had one of my hunches. But I knew then, when I was standing there, talking to Mary Lou Toudahl, that we'd get into trouble with the—the Swamp Wizard. I knew it!"

"Stop that, Cokey!" Jane almost shouted. "There is no such thing as a Swamp Wizard!" Jane told herself that there really was no such thing. It sounded like something out of a fairy tale.

"Oh, isn't there?" Cokey said. "Well there's something plenty wrong around here, you have to admit that. People don't act like these people do, not without some reason, Jane. And, remember, this has been going on—for years. For years and years. The whole village keeps away from the Springs. There must be *some* reason!"

"Of course there's some reason," Jane said through stiff lips. "There's that—that screech we heard. It's a sound that must have been made by someone or something."

"Sound!" Cokey cried, and paced across toward the bed, and then back again to the chest. "That's putting it mildly. It was the most hideous yell I ever heard!"

"But, what I mean," Jane went on, trying to assure not only Cokey, but herself, "what I mean is, we've got to—to find some explanation for that."

"How can you explain the Springs?" Cokey shrugged. "Mrs. Frieson's father said it's been simmering and boiling for—years."

"Well, that must be some kind of a natural force. After all, springs aren't so spectacular."

"But a wizard that lets out a screech when a strange foot is set on the premises," Cokey said, biting out each word, "now that's news, Jane, and you know it!"

They were arguing, and Jane suddenly realized how foolish it was. They were both on the same side—both in the same miserable position. But somehow she seemed more alive and less willing to stay cooped up here than the other girl was. She could see no sense of waiting patiently for the time when they would be freed of their prison. They were going to be free! Of that she was sure. Jane knew in that instant that somehow, by some means of which she was now unaware, she was going to get Cokey and herself out of here—*this night!*

If escape were impossible by way of the window, there were the stairs that led down to the kitchen. It would be too risky for the two of them to go at once and it was up to Jane to go first—to find out if they could get through the door that led onto the porch. It was not far from the stairs. She would need to go past the blue curtain that apparently concealed the entrance to the living room and to the old man's bedroom. After that she would have to walk past the table to the door. It was not far— perhaps only ten feet.

She was so deep in her plan that Cokey's voice startled her.

"The old man kept calling him a boy, but he

must be all of thirty years old. Wouldn't you think he'd have some—some courage? But he's as frightened as they are. Worse, if anything!"

Cokey was talking about Lem Frieson, and the girl was right. Lem Frieson was caught in the grip of terror, completely at its mercy. But there was one thing Jane had remembered about him, which was to his credit. He possessed a dogged solicitude for his mother. The way he had barked at them to go away, not to worry his mother. Jane considered him a poor specimen of a man, but she admired him for being a considerate son.

He must be sleeping now, as well as Mrs. Frieson, and the old man. If her plan were to succeed she must get Cokey to go to sleep, too. That meant that she, too, would have to go through the motions of sleeping.

The fingers of her right hand came up gently to her mouth, as though she were stifling a yawn, and Jane found herself actually yawning. She was tired. It had been a long day, a longer evening. The events of several days had been crammed into the past six or seven hours.

"Oh, but I'm tired!" She said most convincingly, "I'm just dead!"

The yawn was contagious. Cokey's lips parted and her hand came up patting her mouth.

"So am I," she admitted, but shook away the mists of weariness and held her eyes open wide.

"But we can't sleep, Jane. We don't dare!"

"Why not?" Jane went over to the bed and lifted the white covering. There was a quilt under it, thick and soft, a light blue with sprigs of red flowers. Her fingers lifted the quilt, revealing a light cotton blanket.

"Tell you what we'll do," Jane planned, "we'll just take off our shoes and crawl in under the quilt."

Cokey was ready to protest.

"We don't have to sleep," Jane went on quickly. "But at least we—we can relax and keep warm. Our door's locked—and so is the window."

Cokey's blue eyes filled with disappointment and looked at her accusingly. "You mean," she said slowly, "we aren't going to try to get away? We're just going to stay cooped up here?"

"Well, for now—yes. I don't see what else you can do, Cokey."

"We can try to sneak down the stairs."

No, we can't, Jane thought. Not the two of us. I'll have to try that alone. If I can get to the car, I'll come back for you.

"We wouldn't be welcomed," she said aloud. "It might lead to—trouble. After the way they told us to stay up here." She had Cokey's arm and propelled her gently toward the bed. "When it gets light, then we can go, Cokey. They're all too eager to be rid of us!"

And then Cokey said the thing that Jane had
not even let herself consider. But she must have
considered it, or why was she so certain that she
must try to find a way out tonight, as soon as possible?

Near the bed, Cokey stood stubbornly still. *"Are
they eager to get rid of us, Jane? Are they really
going to—let us go?"*

Jane was shocked!

"Why—of course! They—they'll probably shoo
us out without any breakfast. Whether the road is
open or not." She gave Cokey a little shove, so that
the girl sat on the edge of the bed. "Off with your
shoes," Jane commanded, "and get in. You slide
over near the wall."

Cokey sat stiffly. "And leave you on the outside,
near the door?"

"Please, Cokey. I—I'm used to lying on my left
side. Do you mind terribly?"

Why was the girl so stubborn, so set on making
things as hard as possible? It was bad enough to
plan that lonely descent into the dark without having Cokey acting so difficult. But, of course, Cokey
could not know what Jane had in mind.

She said, wearily, "All right. I guess it doesn't
matter. We won't go to sleep anyhow." And then,
bending down to slip off her shoes, "I—I just don't
want anything to happen to you, Jane."

Jane choked.

"Nothing's going to happen to me," she said. "Slide over there on your side."

Cokey had the scarf off, and obeyed with a tired sigh. Jane put the borrowed jacket at the foot of the bed and was ready to lie down when she thought of the lamp. "I'll turn it down, just a little," she explained, padding over the floor in her stockinged feet. "The way that flame dances, it'll hurt our eyes." And keep you awake, Cokey, she thought to herself.

Thankful that Cokey made no objection, Jane put the flame low and remarked casually, "There must be a wind outdoors. A draft comes in from somewhere."

Cokey was looking at her through eyes that she had to force to keep open. "If Moms could see you now," she said, "she wouldn't hold you up for a bright example. You're definitely crumpled."

"It'll wash," Jane said with attempted cheer, pretending interest in her crushed frock. But, of course, Cokey was not thinking, or caring much about how either of them looked. She was thinking of her mother. Her head turned on the pillow, away from Jane. She murmured something like, "Oh, I'll be glad to get back to Moms," and Jane crept in beside her.

"It could be worse," she said, and a long sigh slipped through her lips as her head sank into the depths of the immense, soft pillow. She told herself sharply, "I mustn't go to sleep! *I must keep awake!* As soon as Cokey dozes, I'll get out—and go down there. I've got to keep my eyes open." But, nevertheless, they closed.

"Jane," Cokey murmured, "are you awake?"

"Oh, sure, I'm wide awake." But in the next instant, or what seemed the next instant, her eyes went tight again. She heard the soft, even breathing that was Cokey, drifting into forgetfulness, and with all her will power, she made herself keep alert.

After long, quiet minutes had passed, Jane was certain that Cokey was sound asleep. Now, she told herself, was the time. She eased herself slowly, quietly to the edge of the bed, stood up and reached for the jacket. Cokey stirred, and she stopped, frozen. But the girl's eyes seemed to be glued shut. Jane gave a small sigh of relief and put on her borrowed wrap. For another long moment she stood listening, waiting to make certain that there was no activity on the floor below.

Assured that all was quiet she went to the door and turned the lock. It made a sharp click, and again Jane paused. Cokey murmured sleepily, but did not awaken. She won't, Jane thought, she's dead tired.

So was Jane, but the few moments she had stretched out on the bed had helped a little. She made herself think of the day ahead, and that brought her to her senses, tense and ready.

She stole on tiptoe through the door of their bed-room and onto the bare boards of the long hallway. There would be no light to guide her to the stair-way and past the insecure railing. She must remember not to lean on it heavily.

She closed the door, and darkness covered her. Now, if Cokey would only sleep on. . . .

Step by step, Jane crept toward the head of the stairs. Once a board creaked beneath her feet and she paused; the sound had seemed enormous in the stillness. But the quiet held and after the wild beating of her heart had stopped, she breathed more easily and continued.

At the top of the stairs, she almost gave an audible sigh, so great was her relief. The stairway door was open, and a faint bluish glow came from the window that opened on the back of the house. The moon was bright, and this was a heartening revelation. Everywhere it was night, a clear, bright night. All she had to do was to creep down the stairs, cross the space to the porch door, and go around to the front of the house to the car. After determining that it was there she would come back for Cokey, and they would make their escape together.

If things did not turn out this way—if there should be a slip. . . .

Jane bit her lip. There must be no slip. She would get back, safely. After the heavy rain it was a clear, bright night.

Running her hand along the wall, she slowly descended. As she approached the high, bluish rectangle that was the open door below, she could hear the ticking of the kitchen clock. Except for its slow tick-tock, tick-tock, the Frieson house was wrapped in quiet.

As she reached the very bottom of the stairs, and was ready to make a hasty run for the porch door, a shrill cry suddenly split the night with horror, striking like a physical blow upon her unsuspecting ears.

The cry of the Swamp Wizard!

Jane stood, rooted to the spot, one hand clutching the frame of the door, the other gathering the collar of her frock into a hard knot. Her eyes stared straight ahead, toward the front of the house in the direction the cry seemed to have originated. As though some evil thing were waiting there, blotting out all hope of escape, as though some uncanny intelligence had been aware all along of her intention, the cry had come to her like a signal of warning.

Cokey! what of Cokey? Would the girl awaken? Had she awakened already? Had she missed Jane? Would Cokey cry out?

The house seemed to come blusteringly, wildly alive upon the instant, and Jane thought of her own precarious position. Hide! Hide! She almost whispered the words, while her eyes roamed frantically.

To her left was the curtain—her only hope. She groped for the heavy folds, drew them aside and slipped through into the darkness of a room she had not seen before. It appeared to be the living room.

Voices were rising and she could make out Mrs. Frieson's and her father's. A door to her right opened, and the old man stood there, thrusting his hands into the sleeves of a bathrobe. To avoid discovery Jane flattened herself against the wall, but the old man did not look in her direction. He raced into the kitchen, and met Mrs. Frieson who arrived there at the same time. Jane heard her cry of relief.

"Father—you're safe!" In the next instant, terror crept into her voice. "But—Lem! Is Lem in his room?"

"I don't know! I don't know!"

"His room is right next to yours! Didn't you hear anything?"

"No. No, I didn't hear Lem. Only th' cry. It come again, Alma!"

"Don't stand there, father! Here, take the lamp. We'll go in and see if Lem's all right."

They're going into the bedroom off to the right, Jane presumed. The old man had left his door partly open, and Jane could discern a second door near it. Vaguely she had studied the place where she now found herself. It was a living room, long and divided by a square arch. There was another curtain here, divided and pulled back. An upright

Jane Hid Behind the Sofa

piano stood stiffly in a far corner, and there were several rocking chairs and a low sofa, which was close enough for her to touch. Jane found that she was actually running her fingers over its plush edge. Before she realized what she was doing, she was back of it, crouching on the floor. The sofa was at an angle, and there was room enough to hide.

Alma Frieson and her father continued into the second bedroom.

"Is he in there?" the old man said. "Is he all right?"

"Come away, father," Alma Frieson said, in a sharp whisper. "He's sound asleep!"

"Why, so he is! Looks like he never heard it!"

"Come away now. He's all worn out. If he doesn't wake up, *we* won't let him know."

The old man groaned.

"It might come again. Y' thought it wouldn't, Alma—but it did!"

"Oh, hush!"

"Y' got to admit it, Alma!"

"I'll admit nothing. Only come away from that door!"

It sounded to Jane, hunched over behind the sofa, that Alma Frieson and the old man were moving about, and she could see the light from the lamp, dimly at first, fall in a glare on the floor at the edge of the sofa.

Were they coming directly to her hiding place?

CHAPTER SIX

TO THE MYSTERY POOL

How long Jane crouched there, watching the fingers of light that seemed to grope along the floor, trying to discover her hiding place, she did not know. Her eyes ached from watching the gleam as it danced over the thin, red rug, with its flower design of deeper red. They seemed like living things, these flowers, as though bent and twisted under a heavy wind. The voices of Alma Frieson and her father were still audible. They were standing near the sofa, but talking in whispers. Jane caught only snatches of what was being said. The old man did not want to return to his bed immediately. And his daughter was trying to induce him to do so.

At last she said, "All right. Come back to the kitchen. We can't wake Lem!"

The light moved away from the sofa with them, and Jane felt a tremor of relief. She was not free to relax her muscles, to stand up and enjoy the luxury such a change of position would mean, but the weight had been lifted from her inner self. She had not been discovered!

Jane could hear them moving about in the next

111

room. The lamp was set down, and a single ray of light came through the blue curtain, falling a good two feet from where Jane waited. A chair was cautiously moved, and the old man sighed deeply.

"It come again, Alma," he said in a raised voice. "You got to get rid of 'em, I tell y'! They can't stay around here!"

"Not so loud, father!" Alma Frieson answered.

"Lem's sleepin'," he said. "If that yell didn't wake him up, my talkin' won't. We got t' settle this —once n' for all!"

"It is settled, father. They're going away in the morning. They couldn't go tonight. You know that!"

"I know that th' cry come because they were here! Not once—but twice. Th' Wizard don't want 'em here!"

"Father, please!"

She must have put a pleading hand on his arm, and the old man apparently had shoved it away. Jane bit her lower lip, and held back her very breath as she waited, straining to hear every word.

"Don't try to argue me out of it, Alma! It's your own kin's at stake! For a couple of strange girls, y'd risk y'er own flesh n' blood!"

"That's not true! I don't want them here any more than you do!" Her lips must have twisted, bitterly. "I don't go in for entertaining guests, not any more! But you need not worry. We're all safe, in the house. Nothing will happen to us, in the house."

"Won't it? That cry come *twice*. An' it's because you took 'em in, Alma. Not only let 'em on th' place, but fed 'em and give 'em a bed!"

Alma Frieson must have been seated, but now Jane heard her moving about. The ray of light that came through the curtain flickered, and Jane guessed that Alma Frieson must have picked up the lamp.

"There was nothing else I could do, father. Whether or not I wanted to. I tell you, we're all safe for tonight and I'm tired. I'm going to bed."

A chair scraped. The old man was standing. "Y' can't go t' bed! How can y' sleep, Alma, knowin'—?"

"All I know is that I'm bone tired and I'm going to bed. You can stay here if you want to."

"No. No, I'll go t' bed, too, but y' got t' promise me you'll get 'em out of here th' first thing in th' morning! Promise me that!"

"I promise you!" Alma Frieson said grimly. "I don't want them here any more than you do. Now, please go to bed, father. I'll wait here with the lamp till you get to your door."

He muttered something under his breath, about never being able to sleep, and that they would never live to see the next morning. He came through the curtained way, and the light glared out for a time, farther away from the sofa. A few minutes later, his door was shut, and Alma Frieson was alone in the kitchen.

Jane knew now that the old man and Lem Frieson occupied rooms that led off from the living room. But where was Mrs. Frieson's? The answer came in the light of the lamp. The woman came back suddenly, to stand alarmingly close to the sofa. For an instant Jane had a sickening fear that all along her hiding place had been no secret—that Alma Frieson had come to demand an explanation of her presence there.

The woman crossed the length of the room, however, and departed through the curtained arch that led beyond. Then Jane heard a door close, and all was darkness. The house became quiet again.

Alma Frieson's room was at the back, near the kitchen. A door led from it to a hallway. The woman had come in from the kitchen when the cry had sounded. There was one consoling thought: her room was a good distance from the upper stairway. Jane had not heard that door shut and guessed that it still remained open.

Now she had to hurry back to Cokey!

Had Cokey wakened when the cry had come? Had Cokey missed her?

There had been no sound, no movement overhead, as far as Jane knew. Perhaps Cokey had slept through the excitement, and Jane hoped fervently that this was the case. She hoped, too, that the girl might sleep on, until she could come back to the upstairs room. Then, when they were together, it would not matter.

It was with an effort that Jane stood up. Her knees felt thick and heavy, and her shoulders were stiff. She held to the top of the sofa and raised herself on her toes, repeating the exercise until her legs were limber enough to walk without making too much noise. Then, swiftly she was over the sofa and standing near the curtain.

A sound from one of the bedrooms off the living room caused her to pause. A voice was murmuring, low and fretful.

The old man was tossing on his bed, and Jane heard the creak of the springs. Perhaps he would be coming out again—to find Alma. There was not a minute to lose!

She pushed the curtain aside and groped for the door. The shades in the kitchen were up, and the bluish light of the moon saved her from a misstep. She could see that the door was open, but otherwise the stairs were in complete darkness.

On hands and knees, creeping up a few steps at a time, and then pausing to listen, Jane went up, and the old man did not come out of his room. The downstairs remained silent. Only the clock ticked out a metallic: "Can you? Can you?"

Could she make it back to the upstairs room without any interruption? It seemed that the way was clear—that Cokey had not awakened—but when she reached the upper hall the door at the far end suddenly opened, and there stood Cokey, framed in the soft lamp light.

"Jane, oh, Jane, where are you?" she called hoarsely, wild with terror.

There was nothing to do but run toward her without a wasted moment. She must not permit her to call again lest she waken the house.

"Come back inside," Jane whispered, pulling Cokey in with her. "Don't make a sound. It's all right, just be quiet!"

"Oh, Jane! I woke up, and I thought—"

Jane had pulled Cokey into the room by that time, and was closing the door. She was fully aware of the wild questions shining in her blue eyes, but for a moment she enjoyed the tremendous satisfaction of being with her as she stood leaning against the door.

"Lock it, Jane!" Cokey gasped. "Hurry! Now tell me, where were you?"

"I went downstairs," Jane replied, turning the key in the lock.

"But why? What happened?"

Jane walked toward the bed. Cokey was close beside her. "Oh, tell me, Jane," she begged. "I—when I woke up and you were gone—I almost died of fright!"

"When did you wake up, Cokey?"

"About five minutes ago." Her eyes were still misty.

Obviously Cokey had been sleeping so soundly that she had not heard the second cry, and for this Jane drew a deep breath in gratitude.

But Cokey was consumed with impatience. "Will you tell me where you went, Jane? And why? Something must have happened!"

"No. That is, I went—because I wanted to see if the way was clear. I mean, if the car was still there, and if we could—could get away—now."

Cokey's two hands held Jane's arm. "Can we?" she asked impatiently.

"Not now. Anyway, they really do want us to go." A rueful laugh broke softly from Jane's tired lips. "In fact, we're going to be forced out the first thing in the morning."

"Well, that's good news. How did you find out?"

Jane looked at her guardedly. "Keep your voice down, Cokey. They just went back to bed."

"Oh, I will. Only tell me!"

"When I was down there, that—that cry came again."

"Oh—" Cokey gasped.

"It woke up Mrs. Frieson and her father. They were pretty much upset."

"I should think so!" Cokey breathed. "But where were you?"

"Back of the sofa in the living room. They thought Lem might be out again, but he was in his bed. So Mrs. Frieson persuaded her father to go back to his room." Jane thought of the strained moments while she watched the trailing light from the lamp come so dangerously close to her hiding place and she shuddered. Cokey looked at her worriedly.

"It's all right," Jane assured her. "I heard the old man say that we had to be out of here the first thing, and Mrs. Frieson agreed with all her heart. So, I really needn't have gone to the trouble to try to get us out of here now."

The whole business seemed suddenly such a waste of time and energy, as if it were happening in a queer, distorted dream. The lamp on the chest seemed to throw a gleam that widened and went in and out, in and out.

"Oh, Jane, how brave you are!" Cokey was saying.

"How tired I am," Jane thought. She pressed a hand to her forehead. "Don't fool yourself, Cokey. I was scared stiff."

"But you went down there, all alone! And then —that horrible cry came again! I must have slept right through it!"

"Thank goodness." Jane felt tired, strained and stiff, and the words were an effort.

Cokey stood up. "You must be *dead!* To think I slept all this time."

"It wasn't long," Jane protested dully. "I—I don't think I was gone an hour. I—don't know."

How could you know? When you were closed in an upstairs room in a house like this? In a place where people lived in constant dread—in hateful isolation, afraid of having anyone come near them because there was something in a swamp that screeched and screamed?

But that was all it did—a terrifying screech. People were afraid to be outdoors when it happened, but they felt safe inside the house, and they went to bed the same as usual.

"Let's try to sleep," Jane said, aware of Cokey on the floor at her feet, removing her shoes.

"I should say you will," Cokey said fervently, "and you've got to promise me not to leave this room again! Not without me—Jane."

"I promise you. It doesn't matter. They won't try to keep us here."

That was the thought that brought rest—the Friesons would not try to keep them here. They really meant that. In the morning the girls would leave. They would return to the brown house under the apple trees—to Alice Champlin—to peace, and fun, and cookies.

It seemed but a few moments later that a knock sounded on the door, and Alma Frieson's voice came through the wooden panel.

"It's time to get up. Are you girls awake?"

"Oh, yes." Jane sat bolt upright. "We're awake." She looked over at Cokey. "We're awake."

"Come on down, then," the woman said, and stalked away. Her footsteps sounded along the hallway, and with their receding, Jane really awoke.

"We're—still here, Cokey."

Cokey shoved the cornsilk hair out of her eyes, and sighed. "Yes. We're still here. For a minute, I—I didn't know."

Jane was remembering the events of the past evening, not in detail, but as a whole. It had been a horrible evening, but not hopeless. In the background of her mind, she knew that she had been eager to see the sunrise of this new day.

She said, suddenly, elated, "Cokey! Now—we can go!"

The blond, tousled head nodded. "Let's hurry and get dressed."

They both laughed, but not as they might have done had they been together in Cokey's pretty rose room. They were still at Simmering Springs, where disaster bubbled deeper than happiness, but they were viewing each other, and the small joke they shared helped to start the day on a better key. For they were dressed, except for their shoes. They *looked* as though they had slept in their clothes, and each admitted that the other was a sight. It was a cheerful thought, however, and they bounded from the bed.

Cokey found a comb in the top drawer of the chest, and that helped a little. While Cokey fought with the snarls that had accumulated in the night, she grumbled with something of the old gusto that Jane remembered. It brought up subjects of happier days and little remembrances.

They made the bed carefully, without a wrinkle. Jane pulled up the green shade, and warm sun shone in on the white spread. The room looked almost cheerful.

"I guess that's all," Cokey said. "We can go down, now." She crossed over, in front of the window, and looked out. "No, you can't see the car from here."

Jane had said it was out of sight near the kitchen, on the other side of the house.

Soon they would be going out into the sunshine and into the world they knew and understood. Their fear, and the strange eerie cries of the night, had been stilled by the light of the day.

"Let's go," Jane said, linking her arm through Cokey's.

They walked down the hallway. It was Cokey who remembered to mention the railing. "We mustn't lean on it!" she cautioned, and Jane drew away. Why, she did not know, but the insecurity of that wooden span seemed to put a restraint upon her. It reminded her that they must be careful. Perhaps it was because the hall was darker. The shade on the window at the head of the stairs was still down. The small merriment she and Cokey had shared a few moments ago now seemed to be gathered in mists and blotted out.

Cokey must have felt something of the same impending chill, for her grip on Jane's hand tightened. Her face was pale and grave. In silence they went down the stairs.

The door was still open, but the smell of boiling coffee was their only greeting. The table was set for two, but Mrs. Frieson was not there.

Jane thought fleetingly that the big kitchen might have been a cheerful room. But no place could be called homelike when you felt the need to walk on tiptoe, and you felt it necessary to sneak about to see if the people who inhabited it were present.

"It's nine o'clock," Cokey whispered, "five after."

As Jane simply nodded she saw Alma Frieson coming through the inner door at the far end of the room—the door which they had guessed led to her own room. But Mrs. Frieson carried a jar of fruit, and the girls surmised the door opened to the cellar.

She walked heavily, as though she knew the girls were there, but had no wish to speak to them.

The sunlight that beamed through the windows seemed to lose some of its friendly cheer. Jane and Cokey stood uncertainly near the table, watching the woman, as she went to the cupboard, opened the fruit jar, and spilled half its contents into a white

Mrs. Frieson Brought Some Jam to the Table

bowl. Her movements were jerky and stiff. She brought the bowl of strawberry preserves to the table and set it down. Next she brought two glasses of milk, and then a yellow dish with four boiled eggs. To this she added thick slices of white bread and a plate of butter.

Except that it was in the Frieson house the breakfast could have been perfect. Alma Frieson would not let the girls enjoy it. She wore the same green dress she had worn the evening before, but had put on a different apron. It was stiff and white like her face. As she stopped to look at them, her eyes narrowed, and she surveyed them from head to foot. Jane felt herself shrink inside, and Cokey must have experienced the same sensation.

"You slept all right?" Alma Frieson asked.

"Oh, yes," Jane replied, trying valiantly to smile. Let her think we didn't hear the cry. "We were so tired, we forgot to undress."

"So I see. There were nightgowns in the drawer of the chest."

"Oh, were there?" This was Cokey's piping voice. "We—didn't know."

"I thought I mentioned it."

Well, Jane thought, you didn't mention it. You simply told us to go up to bed. You never did a thing to make us feel in any way welcome.

"Eat your breakfast," the woman commanded, motioning to the table with one hand. "I have work to do."

In strained silence, the girls seated themselves, Jane facing the stove so that she could see the woman moving about. On a chair was a big aluminum bowl covered with a piece of cloth, which looked like part of a blanket. Alma Frieson cautiously removed the cloth, and lifted the lid from the bowl. Jane caught a glimpse of a round, white mound of bread dough.

She carefully replaced the cover and the cloth over it, seeming wholly absorbed in her task, but Jane had a feeling that Alma Frieson was waiting for someone. Jane glanced now and then out the window. The car was still there, and she telegraphed the message to Cokey, who nodded back that she knew it, too. They were both choking down the food, wondering who Alma Frieson expected.

A step sounded on the floor of the outer shed. It was Lem, then, whom Alma Frieson was expecting. She was at the door when he came into the kitchen.

The mother and son disregarded the girls as though they might not have been there.

"You got over all right?" the woman said, looking down at his high rubber boots coated with clay.

Lem Frieson sighed and shook his head heavily. "I couldn't get through."

"Oh, Lem!" Mrs. Frieson cried in disappointment.

"I worked for a good two hours. It's—no use."

Alma Frieson's fingers were twined together. "It's

got to be done, Lem. Do you think—if I came—"

"I tell you, it's no use." He looked weary, beaten. "The bridge is out. No help from that way."

The girls both knew that the bridge was out. What Lem Frieson meant, then, was that the other road to the city was also impassable.

Jane noted a look of dismay in Cokey's eyes, a sudden and alarming expression which she shared.

Was their way of escape cut off? Were they to be forced to remain here—prisoners?

Without realizing it, Jane came to her feet.

"Do you mean the road that we were supposed to take—now we can't leave here?"

Her voice cut through the room, like a whiplash, and the two—Alma Frieson and Lem—whirled to look at her. The man's shoulders still sagged, his eyes were filled with fear, but the woman blazed an open hatred.

"Yes, we mean the road that you should be taking," she answered. "My son says you can't make it." Her eyes went to him for a brief moment, and she added, "Not yet."

"When?" Jane asked the man. "When do you think we can?"

He shrugged drearily. "I can't say for sure. Maybe this noon. I got the water draining out some." He had looked away from Jane, toward his mother. "I got to go out now and finish up my chores."

She nodded, her eyes looking beyond him. "When

you get through, I'll go over there with you."

"There's nothin' you can do. Any more than I did." He went over to the rack on the wall. There was a shelf over it, and he reached far back, bringing out a black cap with a visor. As he put it on, he said to his mother, "My eyes bother me some."

She nodded again, with an absent kind of sympathy, as though she were still unable to face the flaw in her plan, still unwilling to admit failure. "Come back soon as you can," she said, and the man muttered in return and went out through the shed at the back of the house.

When the outer door shut, Jane had a wild impulse to cry out, "Wait! We're coming, too. We're not staying in here another minute." But she caught herself in time. Not that way, she thought. Keep your head, get outdoors, but try to hide your terror.

"Do you mind if we go outside, Mrs. Frieson?" she asked.

"Mind?" The woman's lip curled. "Oh, no, I don't mind. Go on."

Cokey coughed. "Let's go, then, Jane."

"Let's run!" Cokey might just as well have put it. "Let's run for our lives! Anywhere is better than here!"

Jane's eyes glanced across the breakfast table to the woman near the stove. "Unless—" Jane made a valiant attempt, "unless we could do something to help you?"

"There's nothing you can do. Go on!"

No, there was nothing they could do—for **Alma Frieson**—except to leave Simmering Springs, and that seemed impossible. Jane wanted to say, "You're not half as disappointed as we are, not one tenth!" But she held her tongue.

"Hurry, Jane!" Cokey said softly.

The two of them walked the length of the room. Alma Frieson turned away from them as they passed her, finding sudden interest in the pan of dough, as though she could not bear to look at them. It was a lagging, miserable exit, and with a great, deep breath, Jane drew in the open air when they were clear of the house.

"Jane! Isn't it wonderful to be *out* of there!" Cokey said from the depths of her heart. She looked back, over one shoulder. "Honestly, I—I didn't feel like myself in that house!" A shaky little laugh broke from her lips. "I still don't!"

"We'll find a way," Jane said, speaking her thoughts. "There's got to be a way out, Cokey. The sun's so warm."

The sun was warm, and the air was sweet and fresh. Jane felt surer, safer already. There, not twenty feet away, was the sedan. And behind it, the road over which they had come the previous evening. The scrub oak, rusty and bent, blotted out any sight of the bridge. But that, Jane recalled, would be too far to see from here. What interested them,

was the other road, the one to the city—the one
Lem had said might be clear before many hours.

Cokey was thinking of it, too. Suddenly she
pointed to the two ruts that led away to the right
toward the barn. "That must be the road to the
city," she said. "It isn't much to look at, but maybe
it gets wider after while."

It wasn't much to look at—simply twin grooves
in uninviting clay. Across from where they stood
was a big machine shed with red paint peeling from
its unsteady walls. The road past it and other buildings which were scattered about—a shed near which
stood a wagon, its front wheels cramped at a sharp
angle, and a low, square structure with a number of
milk cans standing in front of it. Towering above
all of these was a windmill. Where the road dropped
sharply, the low, long roof of a building which apparently was a chicken shed, was visible, and near
this point an elm tree reared into the picture. Jane
could not see the base of it, but through its trunk
ran a long, deep gash. It seemed little short of a
miracle that with so great an opening in its very
heart, the branches above it could be so sturdy and
so thick with leaves.

Jane's eyes wandered back to look over the grassy
slopes where they were standing. Between the
muddy ruts was a narrow path of grass.

"Let's go down," she suggested, "unless—"

From behind the shed where the wagon stood, Old

Rob suddenly appeared like some kind of an evil genie. He looked older in the light of day and his clothes—a dark shirt, a vest of dull green with gaping pockets, and rumpled, gray trousers—hung on his thin frame. A cap covered his white hair. If the sun made the furrows in his face seem deeper, it also showed a stronger, sharper gleam in his deep-set eyes. There was a determination in the way he walked toward them. From somewhere a great, short-haired dog appeared, raced to his side, and stood there as if waiting for some word from his master.

"You come with me, Spike," Old Rob said, nodding toward the two girls. The dog looked at the girls and pressed a little closer to the man. He seemed to be asking for permission to make a leap, and seemed quite capable of doing so. Never, Jane thought, had she seen a more unpleasant-looking beast.

"You come with me," the old man repeated, with a kind of vengeful chuckle, and the two of them, the bent old figure and the ill-faced brute, came to where the girls were standing.

Fascinated by a premonition of disaster, Jane stood silently, holding the hand Cokey thrust into hers.

"What a mean-looking dog!" Cokey whispered.

"Isn't he?" Jane replied, but she was thinking that Old Rob looked mean, too. Nevertheless, she made a gallant attempt as he drew near.

"Mrs. Frieson says the road is out for the time being," Jane commented. "We can't leave just yet."

"That's right," the old man replied, pushing his cap higher so that his sharp eyes peered at them as though looking over glasses on his beak of a nose. "Both roads are out," he said, "but there's this road here. I kin show y' down this road a spell. You come along with me."

The dog made a wide circle, as though answering a previous order, and came up behind them. The old man was at their side, pointing down past the split elm, toward the barn. "You come along with me," he repeated.

Cokey was at Jane's right, the old man was at her left as the three walked along the grassy mound between the grooves of clay. Jane had the strange sensation of having walked along the path before, in a dream. She tried to capture some of the brightness of the morning, some of the beauty of the outdoors, but what there had been of loveliness when they had first come from the house was soon blotted out again and lost. They were being forced along—they had no choice but to go with the old man.

With all her heart, Jane hoped that she was just imagining things—that Old Rob was showing a sign of friendliness, helping to tide them over their time of enforced waiting.

She looked over at him. He still held his head up

as though he were listening for a distant signal. She knew that he was not being kind, and it was no use to pretend that he was. She heard herself say, with a gaiety that rang falsely, "You can't really show us the farm now, after all that rain?"

He looked at her. "No. I can't. But I can show y' some of it."

"It—it seems to be a nice farm," Cokey put in, as lost as Jane.

"Nice?" Old Rob echoed. "Well, yes—n' no. It has its drawbacks."

On they went, on and on, keeping to the safer ground between the ruts, the dog a constant menace. "What I want y' to see, b'fore y' go," Old Rob said, and it sounded like a threat, "is th' Mystery Pool."

Both Jane and Cokey stopped short.

"The Mystery Pool!" they said as one.

"Yeh." He seemed pleased. "Y've never seen anythin' like it, an' y' probably won't again." The dog came up to the old man's side. Old Rob gave his peculiar kind of mirthless chuckle. "Spike wants us t' get goin'," he said. "He knows, Spike does. He's smart."

Jane's eyes flew from the furrowed face of the old man to that of the animal. A low growl left the dog's throat.

If Mrs. Frieson knew, Jane wondered, would she permit them to be led—*to be forced*—down the path

that led to the Mystery Pool? Would she interfere?
Would Lem interfere?

But they were out of sight, perhaps out of hearing. There was only Old Rob, and the dog, and the
girls.

"Why don't you go then, with Spike, Mr. Frieson?" Cokey asked.

"My name's Hensley," the old man corrected.
"Strictly speakin', I'm not one of th' Friesons."

Did it matter? Jane wondered, and caught a
glimpse of Cokey's white face. The sun was making
a golden halo around Cokey's head, and Jane
thought of the warm, bright sun again. This was the
daytime—a beautiful summer day, despite the rain's
ravage of the night before. Birds were chirping in
the trees. From some place over at the far right, the
grunt of pigs could be heard. There was nothing
strange or mysterious about the pigs.

"I'm not one of th' Friesons," the old man said
again. "Y' might call me an adopted son. But I
know the run of th' place." He chuckled again.
"An' with Alma busy in th' house, an' Lem away,
it's up t' me t' show y' around."

With Alma in the house, and with Lem away!
Was he telling them there was no way out for them?
They were going to see Simmering Springs, the
Mystery Pool.

"All right," Jane said as though accepting a dare.
"We'd like to see the Mystery Pool."

She heard Cokey gasp. But that was the only way to handle the situation, not to let him know how frightened she was, or to let the dog know.

"But you know," Jane added, "we haven't much time. We want to leave here as soon as we possibly can. Lem said there was a chance we could get through in a couple of hours."

"That right? Well, come along, then. We go past th' old elm, then there's a little bridge over th' stream. I helped build it m'self." He turned to make sure the dog was there, and stooped to pat its ugly head. "Come along, Spike."

The strangely assorted little group followed the downward path that led past the great elm, and to the Mystery Pool.

CHAPTER SEVEN

BY ACCIDENT?

Before they came to the little, crude bridge that spanned a sluggish stream, Jane saw the rutted road make a turn to the right back of the large barn. "Oh, that's the city road!" she said eagerly.

The old man had been looking ahead, toward an open leafy place beneath a guardian growth of thick trees. "That's it. That's th' city road," he said pointing again in the direction they were heading. "But we're goin' this way now." His tone was cross, and he acted as if disturbed.

Yearningly, Jane and Cokey looked toward the road they had hoped to be traveling by this time.

"It doesn't look so hopeless, Jane," Cokey said. "From here, anyway."

"It ain't hopeless," Old Rob added glumly. "You'll get to it, all right."

"I'd like to get to it right now," Jane said. Just before coming to the small bridge they stopped. "Would you mind," she addressed the old man, "if we walked over in that direction, and looked around a little?"

The white head bobbed, whether in impatience or anger, Jane could not know. But Old Rob was determined they should first go with him. "After I show y' th' Pool," he said. "Then's time enough." The glint returned to his ancient eyes. "Then's when y'll make double time!"

Spike, the dog, crossed over the bridge, waited a moment, then came back. "Y' see?" Old Rob gloated. "Spike wants us t' hurry on. We cross over this bridge, and then I want y' to stop an' listen." They moved on, over the rough-hewn boards. "Just stop, an' listen," he repeated.

But, perversely, he did not permit them to pause and listen for whatever it was he wanted them to hear. One seamed hand went out in a wide gesture, and he began a kind of tourist guide singsong, a diabolical introduction to the spot, calculated to make it appear at its worst advantage.

"Over there," Old Rob said, pointing to an open space among the trees to the left, "over there's what used to be a picnic grounds. Y' can see how high th' grass is. Th' place hasn't been used for years."

"It—it doesn't look very inviting, does it?" Cokey said, to the old man's evident satisfaction.

"No, it don't!" His eyes gleamed at her. "It's any-thin' else but. Y' can see th' tables, almost rotting apart, an' th' benches. It wouldn't be safe to sit on any of them now. An' then, there's th' snakes."

"Snakes?" Jane said, as both girls drew back.

"Oh, nothin' t' worry you—if we don't go too close. Now, you stand here an' listen, an' you'll hear

"Over There's What Was the Picnic Grounds."

it. Over that way, to your right." That was away
from the picnic grounds. The girls followed his
pointing hand. The dog had come close to the old
man's side and stood like a graven image. They all
stood listening, and clearly they heard the bubbling
of a spring.

"Y' hear it?" Rob Hensley asked. "That's Simmering Springs. That's it, simmerin' and bubblin',
the way it's been doin' since th' time of th' Indians
—since b'fore their time. Listen to it! Listen!"

Softly, with irregular gurgles and spurts the
splashing of the water was heard by the girls. It
grew and it faded, but it never ceased entirely.

"Strange, ain't it?" Old Rob said, after what might
have been only a moment. "Somethin' nobody can
understand." He drew a deep breath, and looked
down at the dog. "Come on, Spike," he said. "We'll
show 'em now." With a thumb, he gestured ahead.
"You come on, now." That was for Jane and Cokey.

They did not obey at once. Jane felt Cokey's
fingers biting into her arm and she turned to the
furrowed face. "What would Mrs. Frieson say—if
she knew we went to look at the Springs?" She
hoped her terror did not reveal itself fully. "She
told us to go away. I'm sure she wouldn't want—"

"Alma?" Old Rob seemed annoyed. "Alma's busy
in the house. An' this won't take long. I'm only
goin' t' show y' this wonder of nature—an' I'm goin'
t' tell y' something about it—somethin' I don't

want y' t' forget!" This last was an open threat. Come along, quietly, he said in so many words, or I'll have the dog help you along.

"All right," Jane said. "But, do you mind going ahead? It's—it's slippery here."

A bank rose before them, where the rain had poured down over the clay soil, spilling a stream of wet earth that ran from shades of deep gold to dark brown.

"Sure," he agreed readily enough. "Sure, I'll go ahead. You just be sure y' follow me!"

Jane nodded, and they fell in behind the old man as he led them up and up through the wet earth. Jane kept her eyes on the ground, unwilling to see the "natural wonder" that lay ahead. Fearful of seeing it, and wanting this unreal sightseeing jaunt to come to an end.

What was in the old man's mind? Why was he insisting that they come with him? Jane was positive that Alma Frieson would not approve, nor would Lem.

The old man had a reason and it was known only to himself. Whatever it was he was in a hurry, and eager to have it over with.

Be on your guard! Jane said over and over to herself, and although Cokey's lips were tightly shut Jane knew that she was thinking the same—Be on your guard! They exchanged a nod, quiet and weighted with meaning.

They would not go one inch nearer than was necessary. What was more, they would be prepared for flight, no matter if the old man should strike out at them, or command the dog to leap. They would be on their guard.

The old man was standing still at the top of the rise of ground.

"There," he said. "There's Simmering Springs."

It was a stretch of water, about forty feet across, maybe twenty feet long, tapering away gradually and flowing under another bridge that ran on the opposite side. Around the pool was a lush growth of low foliage, and all around were the trees, hunched close, totally secluding the place.

"Th' Mystery Pool," Old Rob said, in a voice that was scarcely more than a whisper.

Jane thought that he sounded awed and her own sense of fear left momentarily as she viewed this fantastic marvel. She completely forgot Old Rob and his vicious-looking dog for the moment.

The spring glistened like yellow Italian marble streaked with bright blue, and brilliant red. For the moment, the water, in two places, was churning upward, higher and higher, one of the spots remaining at a low bubble, but the other continued rising, as though from some invisible depth a terrific heat had been applied until the boiling motion of the water became intensified. It churned and foamed, splattering up and up, to a height of almost three feet, then, gradually, the movement subsided. The spot which had been bubbling a minute before, sank down, until the place was undisturbed again. Then, from another quarter, not six feet away, began the same procedure.

"It's—wonderful, isn't it?" Jane said under her breath to Cokey. Wonderful, indeed, but a vastly different wonder than a sunset or a starlit sky. There was something terrible about it, something dreadful and threatening to watch and to hear. As she spoke Jane slipped backward, away from the pool.

"We saw it," Cokey said softly, "now maybe he's satisfied. Now—let's go."

They looked over toward Rob Hensley, who was standing at their left, with the dog at his side. Jane was caught by the animal's attitude—legs planted warily, head down—an apparently unwilling partner in this venture. Perhaps Spike did not want them to go on this tour of exploration to the Mystery Pool. He seemed terrified by the boiling sounds of the water.

A low, pitiful whine broke from his throat and he looked beseechingly into Old Rob's stern, set face. Whatever had brought the old man here, it was not his own pleasure.

He saw Cokey moving away, pulling Jane back with her, and he said harshly, "Wait a minute."

"We saw it," Jane said. "It's—very unusual. But I think we'd better go back now."

The white head shook. "Not yet. I want t' tell y' somethin' about all this. Y' ain't likely t' get another chance like this one. Y' see how that water's simmerin' there?" They had to look again, to watch it. "Well, sometimes it spurts up as high as four, five feet. Y' can hear it from the house on a quiet night, simmering and boiling. It never stops. Never. Day or night. And all around there, all that is— quicksand."

The dog gave a sudden sharp yelp.

Old Rob glared at him. "Shut up, Spike!"

A whimper came, and the dog slunk backward. The old eyes went back to the girls. "Quicksand!" Rob Hensley repeated. "Once y' get in there—y' never get out!"

That was what Mary Lou Toudahl had told Cokey. That was what the villagers knew of Simmering Springs. That was the horror that kept everyone away from this place.

And now, Jane and Cokey were here just as Cokey had predicted they would be. It had been one of her hunches that the Swamp Wizard would be more than a name from a wild, foolish story—a real menace to the house under the apple trees.

Jane shook her head. Her hair was suddenly too heavy, too hot. She pushed it back, and looked away from the bubbling pool, where the sun had come splashing through an opening in the trees. It was the sun on her head, too, that was so warm.

Again Jane thought, it's daytime—there's nothing frightening about the day! Daytime, yet a horror hung over this secluded spot. Even the birds seemed aware of the danger of this forbidden water. Their muted voices came from the distant trees near the forsaken picnic grounds.

As Jane thought of the swamp it occurred to her that the picnic grounds could not be called a swamp. The swamp must be over to the right, beyond the bridge across the pool. That was the home of the—

Old Rob cut into her thoughts, as if he could read them.

"Over there," he said, pointing, "that's it. That's th' swamp."

Jane saw his trembling hand. Beads of perspiration were standing out on his forehead.

"Y' can't see much of it," the old man went on hoarsely. He cleared his throat. "Th' brush hides it. But that's the swamp. That's th' home of th' Swamp Wizard!"

It was a low, wild-looking stretch of spiked grass and thick tufts of green moss. Now and then a gleam of silver shot through the darker places where the water ran. That was the glint of the sun on the water of the swamp.

Jane's thoughts had come back to the sun again, to the light of the day, and she had a wild desire to laugh. Even a wizard would be most uncomfortable in that marshy place! But Old Rob had no intention of letting his spell be broken. Sun or shadow, he was wrapped in terror, and he forced his listeners to his mood. Jane noticed, with a start, that he had come nearer to them.

"Th' Swamp Wizard don't want any strangers here," he said. "Y' understand? No strange foot on this spot!"

Cokey gave a dismal little gasp, but Jane felt a surge of anger.

"If you believe that," she said, "then why did you make us come here? We didn't want to, you know! We want to get away, just as fast as we can!"

The white head nodded.

"That's what y' say. An' I can well believe it. But y' had t' see the place first. Y' had t' *know*—"

"Know what?"

The dog had been lying back on his haunches, his eyes half shut, but definitely frightened of the surging waters. A short, subdued bark came from him, but he shrank again at a muttered command from the old man.

"What did we have to know?" Jane repeated. "Why can't we go—now? We've seen the spring."

"Y' had t' know somethin' about it. Once y' get in there—y' never get out, see?"

"Oh, we heard that already!" Cokey wailed, tugging at Jane's hand. "Let's get away from this horrible place, Jane!"

"Just a minute!" Rob Hensley's hand was on

Jane's arm. "You'll get away, all right—an' you'll stay away, y' understand? You'll stay away!"

Jane faced him squarely.

"What makes you think we'd ever want to come back here again!"

The bent shoulders shrugged. "Y' never know. Some folks never can learn. In your case, I want t' make sure. Y' understand? You'll never come back here again! An'—what's more—you'll never tell anyone about th' place. You'll never bring anyone else here. Y' understand?"

He was gripping Jane's arm, too sharply for comfort. The dog had risen, a muffled growl in his throat. Jane was dimly aware of the animal's approach, but she seemed lost in the glare of the sunken, baleful eyes. She gave a start, and must have moved quickly backward, brushing against Cokey. Or had the old man pushed her? Jane did not know. She heard Cokey's cry, a mingling of terror, lost in the rising voice of Old Rob.

"It's happened to another girl, even though they don't say it. But I guessed it. I have my thoughts, all to myself. You keep away! You keep everybody away!"

But by that time, Cokey had fallen. She was slipping downward, down the clay bank and toward the edge of the pool of quicksand. Jane flung off the old man's hand, almost struck at him to free herself as she leaped toward her friend.

"Jane! Jane," Cokey cried out, "give me your hand!"

"Here, Cokey—here!"

Down on her knees, Jane bent forward, stretching out to Cokey, finding her hand, holding to it tightly against the pull of the slippery clay. "It's all right, Cokey. Take it easy! Crawl back!"

The dog was barking furiously, and Old Rob seemed much more concerned with silencing the beast than in assisting the golden-haired girl. Jane was dimly aware of this, and her fury flamed afresh. The old man was a heartless, ill-tempered brute. She was furious at herself, too, for permitting Cokey and herself to be lured to this treacherous spot. If anything happened to Cokey—!

But nothing was going to happen to Cokey.

"I'm all right, Jane," Cokey was saying, shakily, getting to her feet. She looked back at the pool. "I—I wasn't near it, was I? It seemed—so close."

"No—you weren't near it," Jane said roughly. But she thought, you were near enough, Cokey, near enough, so if I hadn't reached you, in time, you might have slipped all the way. You might have been swallowed in that hateful, boiling water. You might have gone in. And—you would never have come up again. It would have been all my fault! I brought you into all this horrible mess. I took it upon myself to promise a total stranger that I would carry a message for her while your mother was waiting for us. I let you come on this wild-goose hunt. It's all my fault.

Like a young tigress, she faced the old man, and glared into his ashen face. "How dared you bring us down here? How dared you push me like that? How would you like it if I pushed you in there? If you think I'm afraid of you—"

She saw the dog baring his teeth, but fear of him had vanished, too. Her eyes found a stick on the ground. In a moment she had it and raised it threateningly. "Down, Spike!" she commanded. "Down, do you hear me!"

But it was not her voice that quieted the dog, nor the old man's bleating. Over and above the tumult that surged in her heart, Jane became aware of a new voice, and a crashing of heavy feet over the wooden bridge.

"It's Lem, Jane," Cokey called out, like a warning.

"Rob!" he called out as he plodded over the soft ground, one arm upraised, "What's the matter? What's going on?" And before he could get an answer, he snarled at the dog: "Get back to the barn!"

The dog's head sank, and with a swift leap, he started in a wide circle, away from Lem Frieson. Soon as he had safely passed the man, he raced wildly across the bridge, back in the direction of the house. Lem had come up to them. His face expressed horror, as he looked at the old man. "What are you doing here?" he demanded.

Old Rob seemed to age before their eyes. "I—I was tellin' them about th' pool," he said. "About— th' pool."

"Telling us about it!" Jane flared. "I think he was trying to push us in!"

"Push you in?" Lem seeméd to explode, and the old man began a wild bleating. "No! No, I wasn't going to push 'em in, Lem! I swear t' it!"

Lem Frieson's eyes went searingly over the old face, and back to the girls. Cokey's jumper was splattered with the clay, and her hands, which she did not seem to know she was twisting together, were covered with the yellow mud. Jane, too, had picked up the mud when she had knelt down to pull Cokey to safety.

Lem looked from them with a grunt and addressed the old man again, "Why did you bring them down here? You should know better!"

"I did it for a purpose, Lem. I did it for your own good!"

"For my own good!"

The gnarled hands pleaded. "That's right, m' boy. I wanted 'em t' see th' quicksand. It was an accident I took hold o' one of 'em. I wouldn't for th' world—"

The younger man cut in harshly. "All right. Why did you want them to see the pool? What was the use in that?"

The deep-set, old eyes narrowed. "So they'd know. So they'd never come near here again. An' never bring anybody else here!" His hand came up, trembling, as he pointed over to the swamp. "Th' wizard cried out a warnin'. He don't want a strange foot on th' place! They come—and he cried out! They got t' go—forever, Lem! Or—or one of us'll be taken!" His voice cracked. Brokenly, he added, "The next time, it might be you, Lem! It might be you!"

"Stop that!" the younger man almost shouted. "You had no right to bring them here!"

"It was for your own good, my boy! I have no relish of being here. But it wasn't only Rosette. We ain't any of us sure of dear little—"

Before Old Rob could finish, Lem Frieson's hand was up, his fist clenched. It seemed as though he were about to strike the old man. "You keep still, you blundering old idiot!" he cried. "You don't know what you're saying! Keep still—and get back to the house!"

The old man muttered pathetically, repeating that he had done this only for Lem's good, but he might have been talking to a stone.

"Get away from here," Lem thundered. "And keep away!" He faced the girls. "And that goes for you, too. You have no right to be down here. This is —private property."

It sounded so inadequate. "Private property." A boiling pool of quicksand, a dismal swamp. It scarcely required a word or a sign to keep trespassers away.

"We didn't want to come here," Jane said scathingly, "you can be sure of that. And if I'd had any gumption, we wouldn't. I let a dog scare me into coming."

Cokey would not let Jane assume all the blame. "I was—scared of him, too, Jane. He—he's a vicious dog!"

A vicious old man, Jane thought. But Old Rob had undergone a change. He was going over the bridge now, walking slowly, painfully. The dog had disappeared, and the whole place was, for a moment, strangely quiet. There was only the sound of the Mystery Pool, bubbling and boiling. Over the swamp, not far away, there was no sound whatsoever. But it was from there that the sound had come before—the eerie, dismal cry. Jane shuddered and turned to Cokey.

"We can go back to the house now," she said, and then turned to the man. He was staring down at the pool, much as the dog had stared, with a kind of fascinated loathing. "We can go, can't we?" And he came suddenly, alarmingly, to life.

"Yes, go!" he almost shouted, his hand on Jane's arm, pulling her away. "Both of you—go! You should never have come here!"

"Get Away From Here," Lem Thundered

"Don't worry," Jane told him, "we'll never come again!"

Lem Frieson let them go on ahead, and they moved down the bank, and to the bridge in silence. Jane looked down into the trickle of water as they passed over it. It was so clear that the golden-brown bed was visible beneath. More quicksand, she thought, and reached again for Cokey's hand. There was the treacherous quality of quicksand about the strange trio that lived here. This was a farm from all outward appearances. There were animals here. Lem Frieson did his chores. Mrs. Frieson took care of the farm house. She kept it neat, she baked bread. But that was only on the surface. Underneath was a tricky, mysterious undercurrent that drew them all into an unfathomable depth of terror —The Wizard of the Swamp.

They were walking past the big elm, in a heavy, uncompanionable silence, when from the house there came a shrill, high-pitched cry. This was not the same screech they had heard in the night—this was the voice of old Rob Hensley.

"Lem!" he called out. "Oh, Lem! Come quick to th' house!"

CHAPTER EIGHT

THE BLACK CAMEO

Lem Frieson knew every foot of the way about the place—every hump in the uneven, gutted road. He could race along surely, and he did, with an agility that surprised Jane. As he ran toward the house, Lem hopped lightly from one grassy plot to another between the grooves of clay. He had his shoulders back, and he seemed like another person, younger, and more alive. Jane thought of this, fleetingly, and in surprise, but she did not forget that it was something urgent that drew the man toward the house. Something had gone wrong at the house, and Lem was racing to meet the emergency.

Lem Frieson did not intend that they should remain away from it. He wanted them to follow. That was evident when he called back to the girls: "Hurry! Come on, as fast as you can."

The house was no more inviting than it had been before, but Jane had a feeling that whatever it was that had happened, they were in mysterious trouble. This was something real. Old Rob had called out like a man who might have been hurt, and Lem had come running in answer to his cry for help.

It was Alma, Jane guessed—something had happened to Alma Frieson. Lem was worried about his mother. He was deeply attached to her. For the moment he forgot to hunch his shoulders and looked more like a man.

The girls could run, too. When Lem was entering the kitchen door, they were at the outer entrance to the shed. For an instant, they paused. "Oh Jane," Cokey gasped, "what do you think—?"

"I think it's Alma," she said as she opened the screen door. "Let's hurry in."

A washing machine had been placed in the center of the shed. It was a grim-looking thing, with a motor bulging beside it, and nearby was a mound of laundry. Jane hastily drew Cokey aside, and they raced past it, into the kitchen.

It was hot in the kitchen. Heat as well as the fragrant smell of baking bread came in waves from the stove. There was a clean cloth on the table, but no dishes. Despite the uncertainty of the moment, Jane looked up at the clock on the wall. It was ten minutes before twelve. The clock was the only thing in the room that made a sound. A woeful stillness hung heavily, and a sense of loneliness. Alma Frieson was not there. Nor were the men.

Cokey was standing near the door which opened close to the wash basin and the pump. She took Jane's arm sharply, and pointed to the door. "They're down there, Jane. That's the cellar, I guess."

Jane paused close to Cokey and they both listened. The voices came from the cellar. Jane stepped forward and opened the door. Coolness struck them, as their eyes tried to study the dark opening. They heard Old Rob's greatly troubled and irritated voice.

"I don't know, Lem, I tell y'! It must a' been one of her dizzy spells. She come down here from th' hot kitchen an'—"

"Well, come on, get ahold of her. We can't leave her like this. I'll take under her arms, and you hold her ankles."

"It *was* Alma!" Jane said swiftly. "She—she must have fallen downstairs!" The outline of the steps could be made out now. They were narrow and without railing. The steps appeared to be made of stone, but Alma Frieson must have known that way well after all the years she had lived here. It had been because of one of her dizzy spells.

"Oh, the poor thing!" Cokey murmured. "I wonder if we could help them carry her?"

"I don't know. The steps are awfully narrow. I'll ask." The men below were speaking in jerky murmurs, as they carried the woman. Jane called down. "Lem—Mr. Hensley—can we do anything?"

There was no immediate answer, only the sound of heavy footsteps scratching against stone. Then Lem called back, "No. Don't come down here." He paused a moment, said something to the old

man, and called up again, "One of you hold the
cellar door open. The other one turn down her
bed."

"Sure," Jane said eagerly, "we'll be glad to."
She looked at Cokey. "You want to hold the door
while I—" and she stopped abruptly. Lem Frieson
was taking much for granted, asking to have Alma's
bed turned down. How could he expect them to
know where it was? They could only guess that it
was the room leading off the small hall-like space
beyond the kitchen.

"I'm sure that's it," Cokey said. "You go on in.
I'll stay here." Jane wasted no time. The door was
not locked, and as she pushed it wide open, her first
impression was of space. It was a large room, almost
square, with windows looking out onto the fields.
A carved wooden bed was covered with a white
spread, much like the one in the upstairs room
which the girls had shared. There was a bulky
dresser with a round mirror above it, a table, on
which was a sewing basket and a heap of rolled-up
socks. Near the table was a low rocker. But it was
the other door which, for a moment, drew Jane's
attention. That, she knew, should lead into the living room with the sofa. Jane could not repress a
shudder at the thought of the wild, uncomfortable
minutes when she had crouched behind that sofa.

But there was work to be done and no need to
move stealthily now. She had been sent to this room

to prepare the bed and soon its owner would be brought in. She could hear Lem and the old man approaching the top of the cellar steps, but she could only make out snatches of their conversation. Hastily, she folded back the white spread, drew down the top sheet, and plumped up the large pillow. She heard Cokey saying something about the room's being ready and heard the girl's low cry of pity. Lem appeared first, his arms about his mother, who must have been of considerable weight. Her eyes were tightly closed, and her face seemed ironed of its lines of displeasure and fear. It was now quiet, almost attractive.

Jane sprang forward. "Let me help you," she begged, and lent what assistance she could as they placed the woman upon the bed. Lem looked at her, then at Jane, but not as he had stared at them before—as an open enemy. He was thinking now only of his mother's condition.

"She had a dizzy spell," he said with an effort so that Jane hardly heard him. "Been getting them lately. Rob thinks she fell down the stairs."

"I don't think. I know. That's where I found her, at the bottom, all stretched out." Rob was standing at the foot of the bed, wiping beads of perspiration from his head. "If anything happens t' Alma—" With this last he glared at Jane—managing to turn so as to include Cokey also. If anything happened to Alma, he said in so many words, it was all of their doing. He blamed their presence for causing her to have another one of her spells.

But Lem did not openly accuse them. He knelt at the side of the bed. One big hand fumbled over the dark head so still against the white of the pillow. "I—I wish I knew what to do for her," he said, more to himself than to Jane at his side. "But she's a hard one to help."

"Perhaps we could put cold cloths on her head," Jane suggested.

"And take off her shoes and—and maybe if she just rests a while—"

Lem glared at her with the same strange, fearful quality that made her remember they were still on forbidden ground. Ignoring the glance, she moved closer to the woman and as she did so the man rose lumberingly to his feet.

"First, I'll loosen her hair," Jane said purposefully, her hands busy with the hairpins that bound the dark hair. She looked over at Cokey standing near the table. "Get some water and a cloth," she commanded.

The blond head bobbed willingly as Cokey sped out the door. The men remained, silent, watchful. Lem was beginning to feel as Old Rob did, that this was all their doing. Jane tried to ignore them. Her fingers moved slowly, tenderly, and suddenly came away sticky and moist. Lem gave a cry at the sight of the blood.

"She's cut her head," Jane cried, and she thought fleetingly, "Now's my chance to be of service. I must keep cool!" That was the way she sounded—cool, competent. She felt pleased. Above all, she had every intention of caring for this strange, pitiful woman. That was what all these people were—strange and pitiful, though somehow unreal.

But Lem was real enough as his big fingers pulled her away from his mother's side.

"What are you going to do to her?" he asked huskily.

"What am I going to do?" Jane flared, "Why, cleanse the cut, of course—if you have any antiseptic. Have you?"

Old Rob came close. He gripped Lem's shoulder. "Don't let her, Lem!" he quavered. "Send 'em away. Get 'em out of here!"

Jane's cheeks were burning. She ignored Rob Hensley and turned to Lem. "You admitted you couldn't help her," she said, "didn't you? Do you want her to just lie here—and suffer? Why can't you go out and see if that road is open?" Her eyes went to the window. Standing here beside the bed, she could look beyond the field, where the ground sloped downward. That must be the swamp, and near the swamp was the road to the city. "Why don't you do that?" Jane insisted, "instead of wasting time in foolish talk? I—I never tried to hurt anyone in all my life. And, certainly, I wouldn't hurt a woman who's just fallen downstairs—no matter how—no matter how mean she was!" Jane gulped.

"Mean?" Old Rob shouted.

"Yes, mean!" Jane shot at him. "That's what you all are. And—worse than that! We didn't ask to come here. It was a mistake. Can't you understand that? Can't you see that we want to get out of here just as fast as we can? We—we have people waiting for us, too. Cokey's mother is probably worried sick right now, wondering what happened to us."

Cokey was coming in the door at that moment with a basin of water and several towels. The two men had not heard her name before, but they knew who Jane meant. Old Rob paused, his mouth partly open, one hand rubbing against his chin.

Jane glared at him. "You made us waste time going down to that pool! We didn't want to go. We didn't need to be shown that horrible quicksand!" She took a short breath. "If you think we'd ever want to come here again, or bring anybody here— you're out of your mind!"

"There's nothin' th' matter with my mind!" Old Rob retorted.

Jane flashed him a dubious look. "I suppose you just push people in that pool for the fun of it," she snapped.

"Now, now—" Lem broke in. "I'm sure Rob didn't do that on purpose."

" 'Course I didn't! Why should I?"

"He had no right to take you there," Lem argued. "No right at all."

A low moan came from the head on the pillow and Jane turned sharply to the needs of her patient. "We haven't any right—any of us," she said heatedly, "to be standing here and doing nothing—when she needs attention. Please," she looked directly into Lem's twisting face, "can't you believe we want to leave? Can't you go out and fix that road? Can't you do something while we do what we can for your mother? We can try anyhow."

Lem's eyes wandered to the window, to the fields and to the road that lay out of sight. "Well—" he said, hesitatingly.

Cokey came nearer and Jane motioned her to hand over the basin, while she continued talking to Lem. "Haven't you any first-aid kit? Any medicine chest?"

"There's the medicine box," Lem said as he glanced toward the open kitchen door. He pointed a finger at it and said to the old man, "Get it, will you, Rob?"

Old Rob Hensley was still writhing under Jane's accusations, still unwilling to let the girls remain in the room. "You'n I can fix that cut, Lem," he argued. "We don't need them in here."

"I want to go out and see how the road's coming," Lem said shortly.

Still Old Rob hesitated.

"I think they'll do better than we could anyway. And we won't be gone long," Lem added. "You can go with me. Now, get the box."

Muttering under his breath, Old Rob went out as Lem moved backward to let Cokey come to Jane's side. Alma Frieson's eyes remained closed. Her head was a little to one side and her hair was down. In a heap near the pillow were the hairpins. Cokey picked them up.

"Poor thing," she said softly. "Is it a bad cut, Jane?"

"No. I don't think so. But I know what to do —for that." She looked toward the door, waiting for the old man. "Anyway, a cold cloth on her head won't hurt." Jane took one of the towels, wet it, wrung it out and laid it over the forehead. She heard the old man coming in. Lem was saying something to him. Then he gave Cokey the large box.

"I think you'll find everything you need in there," he said with a sigh. "Last time I was in the city, I stocked up. We don't go often, so I buy plenty."

He must have sent the old man out, and he, too, moved toward the door. "I'll see about the road," he said, and paused uncomfortably. "I'll be grateful for what you do for my mother."

In that moment, Jane liked the man. She met his eyes frankly. "We'll do our best," she promised. "And—hurry, won't you? We've got to leave soon!"

He believed her, Jane knew. He really believed that they wanted to go. It seemed incredible that they were having such difficulty in making this understood.

"You'd think we were begging to stay! What's the matter with them anyhow?" Cokey said under her breath now that they were alone with Alma Frieson.

"I don't know," Jane sighed. "But if he can find a way through, he will, Cokey. We'll be leaving soon."

That was a bolstering thought. They would be leaving soon. The hours spent in this bewildering house could be forgotten when they looked forward with that hope in mind. The atmosphere was different here in Alma Frieson's room. The harsh mistress lay helpless while the girls ministered to her hurt, but there was something more than that. The room itself, perhaps. It was a quiet, peaceful room, so different from the woman herself. But, Jane thought, as her fingers worked swiftly and gently, any room in the house would be pleasant, if they would but permit it. They were both gone now—the men. The outer shed door had slammed shut upon them and Jane heard their voices, coming from this side of the house, as they went down to look at the road again. Alma Frieson was gone, too, in a sense. Her dark lashes seemed glued to her thin cheeks, and she never once stirred while Jane finished bandaging the cut.

"There," she said, with a small sigh of satisfaction. "I think that'll be all right. It wasn't very deep." She looked toward Cokey, down at the foot of the bed. Cokey had removed the woman's black, stiff-looking oxfords, and now the girl was holding the sheet ready to bring it up and over their patient.

"I wonder if she was seriously hurt," Cokey said uneasily. "What if she doesn't wake up?"

What if she doesn't? Jane said to herself, "You took a lot on your hands, sending the men out, taking all this responsibility." But what could they have done for her?

"Oh, she'll wake up," Jane said. "She's—got to!"

"Maybe we should call them back," Cokey said, hesitantly.

"No." Jane felt suddenly sure that she was doing the right thing. "Let them go out and see if the way's clear for us so that we can get away from here as soon as possible. That's what they all want most, Cokey. Once we're out of the way, they can live in peace again."

"In peace!" Cokey shook her head. "Not around here."

"Well, what they call peace." Jane noted the sheet in Cokey's hand. "I wonder if we should take off her dress, first." But that would mean disturbing the woman too much. "No," she decided swiftly, "just wait till I slip off her apron. And I'll loosen the collar around her neck."

Jane Saw the Black Locket for the First Time

That was when Jane saw it first—a black locket, rimmed with a tiny line of seed pearls and set in a plain gold frame. At the moment she did not stop to examine it, but placed it on the straight chair at the woman's bedside, along with the medicine box. She hung the apron near it, and still the woman had not moved.

"Let's cover her," Cokey said, with a worried look.

"Just with the sheet," Jane said. "Leave the spread back." She was looking at the black-stockinged feet. The stockings were darned neatly on each toe. The feet were narrow, pathetic, quiet, and Jane had a sudden wish to rub life back into them. Not only into the feet, but into the work-worn hands, and the still face that would frown when life returned to it. When life returned, the woman's eyes would stare rigidly, Jane surmised, but that would be far better than this strained quiet. And then Jane was suddenly afraid—afraid that Alma Frieson might never open her eyes again.

She hoped that Cokey did not notice how her hands shook as they covered the woman with the sheet. Cokey was keyed up, too. Jane stopped and looked at her friend. Cokey's dress was streaked with the clay that had dried in brownish smears, and her hair was a tangle about her cheeks. There was a smudge on her chin.

Cokey returned the gaze, and said, with a pathetic

attempt at humor, "You aren't any prize yourself, my dear."

Jane let the chuckle grow in her tightened throat. It was good to laugh, even a feeble laugh was a relief. She looked over toward the oval mirror and agreed with Cokey. She was a sight.

"You know what I think?" Jane said suddenly. "I think we're hungry. You go out in the kitchen and, see what you can find. I'll stay here."

"Oh, no, I'll stay here with you."

"Please, Cokey." She looked down at the closed eyes. The lids fluttered lightly. Jane felt a surge of joy and immense relief. "She's coming to, Cokey. She'll need something, too. Some coffee. That might help. Or milk—or whatever you can find. Go on out there now like a good girl."

"All right," Cokey said dubiously, "but I'm not hungry."

When Alma Frieson opened her eyes Jane was seated on the edge of the straight chair at her bedside. It was strange the way the black eyes came alive—swift and staring. The cloth was still over her forehead and Alma Frieson reached up and brushed it away. She lifted herself slightly on one elbow, and turned toward Jane. "The bread should come out," she said.

Jane had not been expecting that. "The bread?" she repeated. "Oh, yes. Right away."

Alma Frieson sighed and leaned back. Her hands

dropped to the sheet again. She did not attempt to reach up and remove the bandage. Jane looked at it dubiously. It was not an expert job. She could have done better, but it was not easy to take care of a cut like that in a place like this.

With only that one murmured sentence from Alma Frieson, it was again the house that knew no welcome. Jane stood up, looked down at the woman and saw that she was quiet, and went to the door. "Take the bread out, will you?" she said to Cokey. "Mrs. Frieson wants it out."

"Take the bread—?" Cokey replied. "Oh—sure."

Jane could hear her moving around in the big room, putting something down that made a small clatter, the coffee pot, perhaps. It was good to know that Cokey was there, because it was with an effort that Jane went back to the woman's bedside.

Mrs. Frieson's face looked less pale, and she was breathing evenly. Even though her eyes were closed, Jane knew that the woman would be all right. But a heavy sensation oppressed Jane—sense of impending disaster. She looked out the window near the table, and over the fields. The men were not in sight, but they would be coming back soon. Perhaps they would bring good news. It had to be good news!

And then Jane saw that the black cameo had fallen to the floor. She picked it up, ready to put it back on the chair, but paused to look at it more closely. It was a brooch as well as a locket. The black carved stone in the center opened. Inside was the picture of a girl's face. She was about Jane's age, with wide, dark eyes, looking startlingly straight ahead. The hair was parted in the middle and braids on either side curled up and around the head. It must have been an old picture, or a much-thumbed one, for the features were blurred. Only the eyes were vividly clear.

With a guilty little start, Jane put the locket back on the chair, and in that moment, Alma Frieson's eyes opened again. She looked unseeingly ahead, and her lips began to move. A thin trail of speech came as though the woman were speaking her thoughts. Jane could not understand what she said until she heard the word, "Martha."

Jane came nearer, pressed her hand gently over the cold forehead and murmured, "It's all right, Mrs. Frieson. You were hurt, but you're all right now."

If the woman heard, she did not seem to understand.

"That was the way it was, Martha," she murmured, looking dully at the opposite wall. "She got the train at the junction."

Jane wanted to say something that would bring her back, to tell her that this was Jane at her side, a girl who wanted to help her. But it would be useless. Alma Frieson's mind was reverting to some other time. She was speaking to someone who was not present—to Martha, whoever that might be.

The woman's lips moved again. "She got her ticket on the train. That was what she planned to do. So she must have. And then—and then, you know what happened! You know what happened, Martha!" A cry of anguish broke from the woman. One hand came up to her head as though to ward off a blow. She twisted from Jane's fingers, but the girl kept on with her gentle brushing movement.

"It's all right, Mrs. Frieson. Please be quiet. You hurt your head when you fell."

It was like rain seeping down to the roots of a wilted plant. Consciousness of the present came slowly. Alma Frieson's head turned on the pillow. The misty look left her eyes and they grew brighter, harder, until they seemed to penetrate the girl.

"What are you doing here?" Alma Frieson asked suddenly, as her hands went to the bandage around her head. "What's this thing on me for?"

"You fell down the cellar steps," Jane explained quietly. She tried to smile. "It was a lucky thing you weren't seriously hurt."

"Oh, yes." She remembered it now. "I fell. I felt myself falling." Again she studied the girl. "But what are *you* doing here, in my room? Where's Lem gone to? Does he know you're here?"

"Yes, he knows I'm here. We—Cokey and I stayed here with you. He went out to see about the road.

You remember—we were so anxious to get started."

Alma Frieson came to a sitting position. She refused any help from Jane. "I'm all right," she insisted. "I don't need to be fussed over."

She was still weak, and Jane pushed the pillow close to her back so she could sit up more easily. "Cokey is out in the kitchen," she said just to be saying something—anything to avoid looking into the woman's piercing eyes. She hoped that the men would soon return. "You wanted the bread out, so Cokey took it out. Her name is really Cordelia Champlin. And I'm Jane—Jane Withers." She managed a small laugh. "I don't believe we told you our names before, did we?"

The look that Alma Frieson gave her said clearly that it did not matter what their names were. They were unwanted guests. She said aloud, "What's she doing in my kitchen now?"

Jane masked her resentment of that "my kitchen," and said almost smoothly, "We thought maybe you might like some coffee, or something. Cokey's fixing you a tray."

"She needn't bother," Alma Frieson said flatly. "I'll wait on myself. I'm used to waiting on myself."

"But sometimes it's nice," Jane countered. "When you're not feeling well and—"

"Who says I'm not feeling well? There's nothing the matter with me. I slipped and bumped my head is all." She was sitting up high enough to look at herself in the oval mirror. With one quick motion, she slipped the bandage off her head.

"Oh, please don't," Jane cried, but her words went unheard, blotted out in the woman's sharp cry.

"My locket! Where's my locket?" Her fingers were pulling at the collar of her cotton dress. "Have you seen my locket?"

"Why, yes. It's right here." Jane took the pin from the chair.

"Give it to me!" The fingers were grasping, snatching the piece of jewelry from Jane. "It's open!" she cried, a harsh accusation. "You looked inside it!"

Jane was thunderstruck. "I—I didn't mean to," she faltered. "It came open. I had no intention—"

"No intention!" Alma Frieson echoed wildly. "You're a prying busybody, that's what you are! Coming here in my room, pretending to bandage up my head, while you—"

"Please, Mrs. Frieson, I didn't mean to glance at the locket. I put it right down."

"After you'd looked at it, yes! You had no right to look at it! You understand, you had no right! And to think Lem let you in here! What's come over that boy!" Sobbing in anger, she looked toward the window. "Oh, I wish he'd come! I'd give him a piece of my mind!"

But it was Cokey who came, her blue eyes wide

open and full of wonder at the cause of the tumult. She soon discovered that she was part of it. Alma Frieson flared at her, "And you, too! Poking around in my kitchen! Pretending you want to wait on me! Get out of here, both of you! Do you hear me? Get out of here!"

Cokey looked at Jane and backed away. Jane moved toward the door.

"We'll go just as soon as we can, Mrs. Frieson," she said, holding her hands in tight fists hard against her sides. She tried to make herself remember that this woman had been hurt.

"Go, go!" Alma Frieson repeated, as though her strength was spent. She sank back against the pillow. It was not hard for Jane to realize, and make allowance for her condition.

But that was the reception they had received from the beginning. It should not have been any great surprise, except that Jane burned under the unjustness of being called a busybody.

Cokey said nothing until the door had closed behind them. Then, in a whisper, she asked, "What was the matter with her, Jane?"

"It was that locket she was wearing. It came open, and I saw a picture inside." Jane sighed. "I guess it was supposed to be a secret."

"Huh!" Cokey said under her breath. "What isn't a secret around here?" She nodded back toward the room. "Could you see Lem coming back?"

"Not yet," Jane shook her head heavily. "They're still out by the road."

"Come on," Cokey said suddenly, pulling her along toward the cupboard. "I made a couple of sandwiches. You're hungry."

Jane saw the bread on the cupboard work board. A clean towel was spread out, and the pans lined up with loaves half out. The smell was tempting. Cokey gripped her hand and kept pulling her across the room. "I hope I did it right. Anyway, the sandwiches are swell. I ate part of one already."

Jane knew she was hungry, but even as she bit into the bread, her eyes went back to the closed door of Alma Frieson's room.

"Eat now," Cokey said. "We have a ride ahead of us. They want us to get away, and we'll need every ounce of energy we can soak up."

As she spoke, Cokey was taking big, blissful bites. Jane watched her with a kind of dull wonder. But Cokey had not seen the picture of the girl in the black locket, nor the way Alma Frieson had looked when she cried, "You looked at it."

Jane was drinking the milk Cokey had poured into a glass when the kitchen door opened slowly. Old Rob had come in so quietly that they had not heard him. He shut the door and stood with his back against it, his eyes fixed on the two girls.

"I heard it all," he said harshly. "I watched an' I waited. I didn't go with Lem. Not all th' way.

I came back. Y' see?"

"You heard what?" Jane said blankly. "What do you mean?"

"I know what you did, pokin' in Alma's room. You come here t' pry in our affairs, that's what!"

Jane stiffened. She felt Cokey's hand on her arm.

"Jane never poked in anybodys affairs in all her life, mister. She's not the type!"

Rob Hensley turned to glare at Cokey. "An' you, too! You're another one, messin' around in Alma's kitchen!"

"Why—" Jane gasped, "she—Alma—Mrs. Frieson *asked* to have the bread taken out of the oven. And—we were just having a sandwich. Do you mind?"

"We thought we could get away faster," Cokey put in, "if we took a bite first. You want us to leave here, don't you?"

"Want y' t' leave!" Rob Hensley fumed. "Sure, I want y' t' leave! But y' can't—not yet!"

"Why?" Jane put down the glass. "What do you mean?"

"I mean Lem'd have been back if th' road was open. He's workin' on that low spot. It might take him two, three hours yet, that's what!"

Cokey groaned a long, "Oh!" The remainder of her sandwich went back to the lower shelf of the cupboard.

"But you're not pryin' around down here any

more, worryin' my girl!" A horny finger pointed in the direction of the stairs. "You git on up there, an' you stay up there till I tell y' th' road's clear—y' get me?"

From behind the closed door Alma Frieson's fretful voice came: "Is that you, dad? Come in here!"

"I'm comin'," Old Rob said grimly, "in just a minute." He stood glowering at the girls.

We might as well wait up there as anywhere, Jane thought. Perhaps it won't be that long. Perhaps he's wrong. She and Cokey exchanged a glance, and moved almost as one toward the steps. Jane could feel the old man's eyes stabbing them. She knew it would not be two hours—nor three. Leaving Simmering Springs would not be as simple as that!

CHAPTER NINE

SOMETHING NEW

Cokey had not wanted to go back to the bedroom, with its forlorn picture of *Hope*.

"It's bad enough to be cooped up here," she protested, "where we have to wait, not be able to hear anything of what's going on."

But at least they could see something of what was happening on the outside of the house, and Jane pointed this out, as they stood near the window at the head of the stairs. The window looked out over the same portion of the fields as Alma Frieson's. They were directly above her room.

"It could be worse," Jane said, trying to be convincing.

"Maybe," Cokey sniffed. She half knelt, half crouched, to peer out toward the road. "I don't see a thing, nothing moving, anyhow. There's the swamp over there, some of it, and some of the road, but no sign of Lem!"

There was no sign of Lem. Jane followed Cokey, sitting on the floor near the low sill. With one elbow resting on the sill, the fingers of her hand went up and over her chin. She did not want Cokey to see her face. She was thinking of the queer hunch

177

of Cokey's. At the time it had seemed so absolutely ridiculous. Under the apple trees, talking to Mary Lou about a Swamp Wizard and a place called Simmering Springs, Cokey had felt a forewarning of an intangible menace. Jane had tried to laugh away her friend's fears, which had seemed so foolish and far-fetched. She had accused Cokey of making mountains out of molehills. Even the molehills seemed very distant then.

But now Jane had experienced a hunch. She had felt the cool brushing of dark wings over her head, and she had the strange, puzzling fear that Cokey had experienced. Jane's strange thought had first come in Mrs. Frieson's room not fifteen minutes ago when she had looked into those startling eyes in the black cameo locket. Now, the unknown girl would not leave her thoughts. It was not entirely because of the way Alma Frieson had snatched the locket from her hand. She had seemed so horrified that Jane had looked at the picture. It went even deeper than that. In some unexplainable manner Jane felt certain that the girl in the locket would be linked in trouble with them—with her and Cokey.

Jane shrugged, trying to blot out the lingering picture of the wide eyes. Suddenly she saw Cokey looking at her, and she was vaguely aware that Cokey had spoken.

"Huh?" she said. "What did you say, Cokey?"

"I asked you to tell me some more about the picture in her locket."

Jane was startled. Had she spoken her thoughts aloud? Cokey was thinking of the same thing, that was all.

"It was the picture of a girl. A girl's face. You'd think I'd committed a crime looking at it."

Cokey gave a deep sigh. "It's a crime to breathe around here! You feel watched and hunted. I tell you, Jane, if we ever get home again—"

"If we ever get home! We'll get home all right!"

"Oh, sure." Cokey looked out toward the road again. There was silence. Cokey stared directly into Jane's face. "I can't make them out, can you?"

She meant the people who lived in this lonely house. Jane shook her head. "I don't think it'll do much good to try, either. For a while I thought Lem was almost human. I mean, when he said he'd be grateful for what we could do for his mother."

"Yeh," Cokey said in thoughtful agreement, "but old Rob Hensley. Wasn't that something, the way he came crashing in on us, chasing us up here?" She moved restlessly. "I've got a notion to go on downstairs again. I don't hear anyone down there, do you?"

"No—wait." Jane put a hand on her arm. "Lem will be coming back. He'll call us down. The old man will do what Lem says."

It was Cokey's turn to shudder, "Yes, I guess it's better to wait up here. Do you think he really meant to push us into the pool?"

"I—I don't know," Jane said slowly. "I'd hate to think so—"

"But it looked that way, didn't it? He practically forced us to go down there, with that beastly Spike ready to bite us in two."

Jane was looking toward the road, the empty road that wound around the swamp and then was lost to view, but she was not seeing it. She was thinking of the way Cokey had looked, slipping down in the moist clay, of how near she had come to slipping all the way into the treacherous quicksand.

"He said he wanted to make sure we'd never come back here again," Jane said, trying to make the explanation plausible to herself.

"As if we ever would!" Cokey blurted. "Or bring anyone else here!" She laughed shakily. "It's almost funny!"

"Almost, but not quite," Jane said thoughtfully, "Lem was angry at him for taking us down there. And did you notice the dog, Cokey?"

"You mean the way he crouched on the bank?"

"Yes. He was terrified. You could tell he didn't want to go near that quicksand."

Quicksand. The word went over and over in Jane's mind. Treacherous sunken places, far out of sight. Smooth and safe on the surface, but underneath like the things that went on in the minds of the three who lived in this house. Underneath was

"As If We'd Want to Come Back!" Cokey Said

mystery and danger and terror. Why were they so afraid? Was it because of the Swamp Wizard? Who was the Swamp Wizard? Had anyone seen such a person or being? The answer, so far as she knew, was in the negative. No one had ever seen the Swamp Wizard. This was some mysterious being who had been at Simmering Springs, in the swamp land, since the days of the Indians. When a strange foot was set upon the place, that unearthly cry came from the swamp.

But it had not always been that way. There had been a time when the Frieson farm was a happy place. Alma had wanted it to be pleasant. She must have, because she had fixed up that picnic ground. Jane shook her head as she thought of it as it looked now—rotting tables and benches, the unkempt grass.

"A penny," Cokey said.

"They aren't worth it. I was thinking of that picnic place."

"Ugh!" Cokey shrugged. "I thought Rob Hensley would start pulling snakes out of the grass next!" Her fingers twisted together. "He's about the meanest old man you could ever imagine!"

Jane silently agreed. Old Rob Hensley was mean. But there must be some reason for his meanness. They had never done anything to harm him, except to come here. So his meanness grew out of his fear. And his fear. . . .

It came back again to the Swamp Wizard. A circle

that ended where it began, with nothing but fantastic fears.

"But he does think a lot of Mrs. Frieson—and Lem," Cokey put in. When Jane looked at her questioningly, she added, "Old Rob, I mean. That's about all you can say for him."

"I wonder how Alma is now," Jane murmured anxiously. "I wish he hadn't sent us away. But I think she's all right."

"The way she flared at you," Cokey said as she came suddenly to her feet, "I'd say she was good as ever. If you can call that good."

"For a while I was afraid," Jane admitted. "I thought maybe we should have kept the men there. We had a lot of nerve offering to take care of her alone."

"Well, don't worry about that," Cokey brushed the matter aside. "Alma Frieson's the tough kind. She can take a lot of punishment. She'd have to, to live in a place like this!" Cokey was looking out the window. "Oh, when will Lem come!" she said in a burst of impatience.

Jane stood up beside her and they looked out the window together. One of Jane's arms stole about Cokey's waist.

"I'll tell you what, Cokey, we'll get out of here this afternoon, if we have to swim out!" This afternoon! She wondered what time it might be. Two, maybe three o'clock. Her mind went back fleetingly to this same time yesterday. She was on the train, coming to the village of Burley to visit Cokey and her mother. It was almost a whole day since she had first greeted Alice Champlin at the train. How Alice must be worrying! She must have had a horrible, long night of waiting for them through the storm. After the storm there were the long hours of waiting for their return, for a message.

"If we have to swim, Cokey," Jane said again, "we'll make it!"

Cokey's lower lip began to tremble, but she made an effort to smile valiantly. "If Eddie were only home—" she began drearily, but broke off, pushing the wisp of hair from her lips. "But you know Eddie. He's never there when you really want him."

Jane remembered. "You said he went to the city, didn't you? To get a tractor?"

"Yes. And he probably did, but he should be home by now, telling Moms not to worry and everything's just dandy and that I'm always in some kind of scrape anyway." Cokey began to pace about the narrow hallway as though she could no longer bear to remain quiet. Her eyes rested on the door at the left of the steps. "I wonder what's in there," she said suddenly, and walked over, putting her hand to the doorknob.

At that instant the door at the foot of the stairs opened abruptly. Before either of the girls were aware of the woman's presence, Alma Frieson called out sharply, "Are you still poking around in my house!" It was not a question but an open accusation and the girls whirled to look down at her. She stood like a grim statue, hands clasped over the white apron which again covered the green dress. The collar was in place, the black brooch was at her throat. The bandage was gone from her head, and her face was a grayish color, but otherwise she showed no sign of her recent fall.

Jane agreed that Cokey was right. They didn't need to worry about her.

When they remained silent, the woman said: "You'd better come down here where I can keep an eye on you."

"I—I'm sorry," Cokey blurted. "I—got tired of waiting. I just wondered—"

"Never mind trying to explain. Come on down here. Both of you."

"Certainly," Cokey said in a quaking voice, and the two went on downstairs. It seemed they moved like clumsily handled puppets and made a great deal of noise. It was because of Alma Frieson. In the face of her grim disapproval, nothing could be right or graceful. As they came near her, she stepped backward, almost as though she feared they might touch her. They were again in the big kitchen, and Alma Frieson closed the stairway door after them.

They waited near the table in patience. The wom-

an said, "Lem wants to talk to you," and motioned
with a stiff nod toward the stove.

"Lem?" Jane could not suppress the hope that
welled in her heart.

"Oh, Lem!" Cokey burst out excitedly, "is the
road open now?"

They looked into his face as he stood across the
room, and he did not need to tell them that the road
was not open yet.

The man shook his head. "It's no use," he said.
He took off his cap, rubbed the back of one hand
across his forehead. "Not yet, anyway," he added.

They could find no word to say in that moment.
They kept looking at him. His clothing was covered with sticky clay.

The door near him opened, and old Rob Hensley
came in from the shed. He looked over at them
furtively, and it was evident that he knew, too. Perhaps Lem had already told him. Perhaps he had
also been told to hold his tongue, for it was in silence that the old man walked over to the hooks
above the couch. Slowly he hung his hat there.

Alma Frieson's voice penetrated the silence. "You
better take your nap now. It's after your time."

"Yes, yes," he spoke fretfully, but moved toward
the girls, went past them and beyond the blue
curtain.

As though they were not there, the woman went
over toward the cupboard and busied herself with

a spoon and a bowl, keeping her back to the girls. Lem was watching her, a frown cutting through his forehead.

The word "quicksand!" came swirling through Jane's head again. Everything was real enough on the surface, but underneath were treacherous, dark places. Alma Frieson made no secret of her bitterness toward them. The woman's dislike was as evident as the wild gurgling of the pool as it boiled up in the sun. But Lem seemed different. He was trying to smooth the way somehow, trying to pacify them and his mother, too, but it was no easy task.

After what seemed an age, Jane found her voice. "But the road has to be open!" she said. "We have to leave here! It's—" she looked back, at the clock on the wall. "Why, it's after three!"

The spoon in Alma Frieson's hand scraped gratingly against the side of the bowl.

"I know, but I tell you, I did all I could!" Lem argued as he glanced toward his mother's straight back. "It's no use," he said. "I know that clay."

"But haven't you got horses that could pull us through?" asked Cokey, moving over toward him. "Or maybe that we could ride?"

Lem Frieson shook his head. "You might not make it. Something might happen to you—"

This unexpected consideration was so great that Jane gave a start. "Why, if we could just get a lift over the worst place—"

"It's a mile stretch," Lem pointed out. "All along the swamp."

Jane and Cokey exchanged a long, meaningful glance. "All right then," said Cokey, suddenly. "We'll swim back!"

She meant it, and Lem Frieson knew it, but his reaction was more surprising than his first show of sympathy. "You couldn't do that!" he cried in alarm. "Why that river's whirling along. You might—! No, you couldn't take that risk. I wouldn't let you!"

Alma Frieson, holding the bowl and the spoon, turned to look at him. "Why can't you let them?" she asked flatly. "If they want to go, let them go."

"They'd never make it!" Lem insisted.

The woman shrugged. "I've made it. I swam that river already."

"Not the way it is now," Lem said stubbornly. "They can't try it. They'll have to make th' best of it, that's all."

Alma Frieson had put down the bowl. She seemed to have ignored the girls as though they were not in the room. "What do you mean, Lem?" she said slowly. "Make the best of it?"

"Why, wait, that's all. Wait till the bridge gets fixed, or till the road's safe. It's too much of a risk yet."

Jane and Cokey looked at each other in bewilderment. To have Alma Frieson want them away as soon as possible was to be expected, but to have Lem be so considerate, to have him suggest that they remain, that was something new, something they could not quite understand.

Alma Frieson was talking bitterly to her son. "Too much of a risk! And what about us? Have you thought about that? What about us?"

Lem's shoulders were sinking again. He looked very tired and his voice was weary. "We'll be all right."

"Oh, will we?" The woman was controlling herself with an effort. "After last night, you say we'll be all right! You heard it, Lem. Not once—but twice. It came twice!" The girls could scarcely hear the last words. Her voice sank to a hoarse whisper. "You might—" she began, but Lem went over to her and put one hand clumsily on her shoulder.

"I'm sure it'll be all right. And, maybe, it won't be they'll have to spend the night." His eyes went out the window, where the car was standing. "There's a good wind and the sun's hot. I'll go back again in another couple of hours and see."

"Another couple of hours!" Alma Frieson scoffed, as though in that length of time there would be little or no hope for any of them. As though it would be too late then. They would all be doomed together.

Lem's expression changed. He seemed provoked. "I'm doing my best," he said shortly. "This is no fun for me, either. I've got work to do, too." Alma

Frieson was leaning against the cupboard. Lem's expression softened. "You should be in bed," he said clumsily, looking at the bowl on the wide shelf. "Why don't you let everything go and lie down?"

"I'm all right," the woman said gruffly. "Go take care of your work. I can manage here."

Lem bit his lower lip, regarding his mother for a long, silent moment. Then he turned to the girls. "I'll come back in a couple of hours and let you know how things are," he said rather unconvincingly without looking at them directly. "You better stay in the house and wait."

"They'll stay in the house," Alma Frieson said in a tone that was more than a promise. Lem went out the back door and soon the door of the shed slammed shut. Alma Frieson pointed to the couch under the row of coat hooks. "Right there!" she said. "Sit there, and stay there—both of you. There'll be no more poking around in my house."

"Oh, we weren't, Mrs. Frieson!" Jane said swiftly, but the pointing finger grew sterner.

"Sit down there, and keep quiet! And don't think you can fool me. I'm all right now. I can keep on my feet. You do as I say."

She was on her feet, but it must have been with an effort. Jane thought of what Lem had said. His mother was a "hard one to help."

Cokey had not wanted to wait upstairs. She preferred to be down here, where she could see and

hear better. For that matter, so did Jane. Unpleasant as Mrs. Frieson was making the situation, the
kitchen was preferable to the upper bedroom. That
room beyond the shaky stairway railing was like a
prison.

It was Cokey who said: "Why, sure we'll wait
here." Her hand found Jane's and gave it a tug.
They went together to the couch and sat down.

Alma Frieson stood where she was, regarding
them with a long, stony look that made them uncomfortable—almost unbearably so. Her set lips
parted suddenly. "I have to go down to the cellar
for eggs," she said. "Don't you move from there."

Jane observed one of her hands reach back of her
to grasp the edge of the cupboard. Alma Frieson was
feeling the effects of her fall, stern woman that she
was. Jane came to her feet.

"Please, let me go, Mrs. Frieson," she begged.
"You're hurt. You might fall again!"

"I won't fall again." Her face was deathly white.
She moved slowly over to the rocker and after seat-
ing herself, held firmly to the arms of the chair.

Cokey was beside Jane now. "She ought to go
back to bed, Jane," she said. Steps were heard behind them, and they turned to see the old man
coming through the curtained entrance.

"You leave her be!" he rasped at them. "You git
away from her an' leave her be!"

"But she's weak from that fall," Jane protested.

"She should be in bed!"

"It's none of your affair!" Rob Hensley snapped, as his shaking finger motioned them back to the couch. "You sit where she told y' an' mind your own affairs. I'll take care of my girl!"

Alma Frieson's head rested against the back of the chair, and her eyes were partly closed. Old Rob put an arm under her shoulders. "Come with me," he half urged, half pleaded. "You lie down a little while an' you'll be better. Come, now."

Strangely, the woman obeyed him and the two moved slowly across the floor, past the cellar door, to Alma Frieson's room. The door closed on them.

"What's the use, Jane?" Cokey sighed. "You can't help people like that."

"I guess not," Jane admitted. Her eyes surveyed the kitchen. "I wish she'd let us do something. It's so—useless, just sitting here—waiting."

Cokey looked toward the woman's room. "We'll have company, I'll bet. The old man will be coming back to see that we obey orders."

"I suppose he will. To see that we don't poke around! Well—"

They went back to the couch. The clock ticked loudly. From beyond the closed door, there came a low murmur of voices.

"Do you think we should try it, Jane?" Cokey said suddenly, in a whisper.

"I—I don't know." Jane's hand pressed to her

The Two Moved Slowly Across the Floor

forehead. It had been such a long, long day—a day which was by no means over yet. But the strangeness that grew with each passing hour had made the minutes stretch beyond time. This was an experience Jane could not even have imagined. This strange house and its inhabitants were as remote as though they existed in another world. And yet, Jane thought, how near they were to the things they knew—the village and the brown house under the apple trees.

She tried desperately to control her pounding thoughts. She forced herself to think clearly.

"It's not far, Cokey. To your house, I mean."

"No, only seven miles." They had said that before —*only seven miles*.

"The way we came might be the best bet," Jane said, "if it weren't for the river."

"Lem seems pretty sure it wouldn't work." Cokey's hands were tightly clasped over her knees. She, too, was trying to straighten out the twisted maze of thoughts. "Swimming's out. It's funny about him, isn't it. He seems to want us to get back safe and sound."

It was funny about Lem Frieson's solicitous interest in their welfare. But, Jane thought, he had not wanted them to be near the Mystery Pool either. He had been furious with the old man for taking them into the face of danger. Lem had never wanted to hurt them. He had wanted them to leave as soon as possible. They all wanted them to leave—and the girls yearned to be away from the place—but getting away seemed impossible. The river, the road, and the swamp were impassable barriers.

Jane's hand went to her forehead and pushed back her dark hair. "I can't just sit here and wait, Cokey!" She leaped to her feet. "We've just got to do something!"

The door to Alma Frieson's room opened and old Rob Hensley came out. A quick look at him told the girls that he had heard Jane's words and they decided that they had better be quiet. He shut the door gently behind him, paused before it for a moment to listen, and then came to stand before the girls.

"How is she?" Cokey asked him.

"Restin'," Old Rob said in a whisper. "An' you be quiet now."

"We won't make a sound," Jane promised in a voice that seemed unreal even to her own ears. "We'll just sit here for hours on this couch and wait!"

The old man looked at her quizzically. "That's th' idea," he said.

"Sure," Cokey confided. "You know how it is. You went to take your nap, didn't you? Only you forgot to go to bed. You stayed behind that curtain to find out what was going on!"

A gleam came into the man's sunken eyes, a glint

that was almost the ghost of a twinkle. But a hand came quickly to cover his mouth, to wipe away anything that might resemble a smile. Had he really been ready to smile? If so, it was an almost incredible gesture.

He looked at them grimly. "What I do's my business here. And what *you* do is my business. You wait now—an' listen!"

They waited and they listened. Old Rob went to the window near the stove. He leaned close to the screen and called softly, "Spike!" There was no answer at once and he repeated, "Spike!"

A low sound came from outside. Spike was there, waiting for orders. "Stand guard, Spike," Old Rob said. "Stand guard!"

A growl came from the dog as if he were promising obedience. "Good Spike," Old Rob applauded, and turned to the girls. "Y' heard that, didn't y'? Spike's standin' guard out there. So y' better not try any foolishness. It won't go well with y' if y' do!"

Cokey shrugged and sank back to the couch. Slowly, watching the piercing, unblinking eyes, Jane sat beside her. Finally satisfied, old Rob Hensley gave a grunt and made himself comfortable in the rocking chair. Jane was still watching him through a kind of haze, and her thoughts were reeling dizzily. One thought emerged from all the others and stood out like a dread warning: "Once you get in, you never get out!"

CHAPTER TEN

COMPANY

How long they sat there on the couch, Jane did not know. Minutes dragged along endlessly, ticking loudly on the clock over the table. There were other sounds that broke the quiet; the creaking of the rocker as the old man moved back and forth, one foot crossed over the other. With one substantially planted foot on the floor, he made the chair move gracefully back and forth. The old man was obviously prepared for as long a wait as necessary until Lem should come back. At the same time he seemed to be enjoying himself. Now and then he would look out the window where Spike was standing guard. Occasionally the dog growled, perhaps when an insect annoyed him, or when he presumed that all was not well.

Once, when the dog had uttered a low snarl, Cokey whispered: "How he'd like to get his teeth into us!" She was sitting hunched over, her hands making small fists. "Oh, how I wish Lem would come back!"

The old man glared at her, and said in a hoarse warning, "I told y' t' be quiet! Alma's sleepin'. She needs her sleep."

Cokey sighed, straightened, and tried another position, leaning back against the wall. It must have been more comfortable, for she drew Jane back. The clock ticked on and the old man rocked and rocked. Now and then the dog growled.

They drifted off into sleep, but Jane did not realize it until she was awakened by a sudden, loud sound. Before she knew what it was, she felt something soft across her face. It was Cokey's hair. Cokey had been asleep, too, but had also been awakened by the sound.

"What—happened, Jane?" she said dazedly, as the sound was repeated.

It was Spike, the dog, barking wildly, furiously.

"Be quiet, Spike!" Old Rob said, bending near the window. "Be quiet, I say!"

A whine came in answer, a low, pleading cry, and another muffled bark. "I'm comin' right out," Rob Hensley told the dog. "Not another yip out of you!"

He moved toward the door, but turned back. "You stay right where y' are!" he said, and then he went out the door.

The girls were both wide awake by this time. "Now what?" Jane said, "It can't be Lem coming back."

The outer screen door slammed shut.

"Look at the time, Jane! It's five o'clock!"

Incredible as it seemed, it was five o'clock! The afternoon was almost gone. Jane pressed Cokey's fingers. "Let's go over and look out the window."

They waited by common consent for the space of a minute, making sure that the old man would remain outdoors. He was talking to the dog, asking him what was the matter. "Let's go," Cokey said, and they rose stiffly, and went to the window.

Old Rob was standing out there in the yard, with the dog at his side. They were looking down the road that led to the oak trees—the road over which the girls had come to the Frieson house. They could not see much of it from the house, but the old man and the dog could see, and they were standing there like two statues.

"Don't you make a move," Rob Hensley commanded the beast, when the dog began to growl again. "Back, Spike! Down!"

The dog retreated a step, but remained standing at rigid attention.

Finally, after what seemed an endless wait, the girls heard voices in the distance. A man called out a greeting. Then a woman's voice repeated something similar.

"Oh, Jane," Cokey said, "do you suppose somebody could be coming—for us?"

It seemed too good to be true, something they dared not hope. "We'll know pretty soon," Jane answered. "I can hear them walking over that little bridge. They're almost in sight."

Cokey's hand was on Jane's shoulder, but Jane

scarcely noticed. She was all eyes and ears, straining every sense to see who it would be.

And then two men and two women broke into view. One man had his hand upraised, as if he were greeting Old Rob or asking a truce with the dog. Jane did not know which. He was a stranger, as was the second man, and the large, tall woman. But the neat, slender figure in the plaid suit could be no other than Alice Champlin!

Jane heard Cokey's deep-drawn breath and then the cry that she would never forget. "M-M-Moms!" she cried, trying to believe her eyes. She pointed wildly to the window, begging Jane to verify it—to assure her that it was true.

"It's—Moms, Jane! See? It's—really and truly Moms!"

"How did she ever get here, Cokey?"

"I don't know," Cokey said in reckless happiness, "and I don't care! She is here!" She was about to rush away from the window, toward the door to go out and welcome her mother, when old Rob Hensley on the outside of the house turned to glare in at them.

"You stay in—" he began.

"My mother's out there," Cokey shouted, "you understand? And if you let that dog hurt her—"

"Your mother!" Old Rob said as though he had thought so, but was greatly pleased to be certain. "Don't worry. Spike won't hurt her." To bear out his word, he said to the dog, "Down, Spike. Down!"

Cokey gave a breathless sigh, then took Jane's hand. "Let's go out to meet her. Let's let her know we're here."

"She knows already," Jane said with soaring delight. "She saw the car."

"Oh, sure! That says it, doesn't it! Oh, Jane— to think—to really and truly think—" Cokey said no more. They raced out through the shed. Even in the glow of their sudden release, Jane remembered the mound of laundry. She was ready to hold Cokey from stumbling over it, but the washing machine had been pushed back, and the laundry was gone. Jane thought fleetingly of Alma Frieson. Could she, after a fall like she had, remember to clear it away? But another, a brighter, sweeter, personality claimed her full attention—Alice Champlin! They were going to meet her—now!

Old Rob Hensley had kept his word. He and the dog stepped back in the path and cleared the way for the meeting. Jane let Cokey rush ahead. There was a tangle of silken hair, as arms flung out wildly. Like the little girl that Jane remembered, Cokey was wildly hugging her mother.

Alice Champlin laughed, and what a wealth of meaning was in her pleasant voice. "Oh, Cokey!" But she did not forget Jane. Her eyes were looking over the blond head, to Jane's. She got one hand free and Jane grabbed it. "And—Jane! Oh, you're both safe! I'm so happy!"

"I guess we are, too," Jane said shakily. "We thought maybe we'd have to stay another night."

Cokey was babbling. "How did you get here, Moms? How could you get through?"

"Where there's a will—" Alice Chaplin said, and turned to old Rob Hensley. "I want to thank you," she said with a gracious smile, "for being so kind to my girls."

The old man grunted something, but Jane was still too wrapped in bliss to consider how mistaken Alice Champlin was regarding the old man's true character. Her rubber boots were muddy almost to the tops, and Jane could see that Alice's trip had not been easy. She had made it, but how?

And these other people? Had they come with her? Who were they? In the next instant Jane recognized the tall, big-boned woman as the one who lived in the house on the hill, but Jane was certain she had never seen the man before.

Presently she became aware of an unnatural quiet among the group. Alice Champlin had spoken her thanks; the old man had muttered a reply, and there the talk had ended.

Jane scrutinized the large woman. She saw the wary expression in the pale eyes as they went quickly over one shoulder toward the split elm. Her shoes were muddy, too. Then Jane hastily appraised the two men standing near her. One was a lean, weather-beaten figure in overalls which were stuffed into high boots. The other was a younger man, stout and ruddy-faced. He leaned closer to the large blond woman and whispered something in her ear. She nodded, and both glanced toward the barn.

Then Jane knew—the Mystery Pool—of course.

Alice Champlin seemed to sense, but not to fully understand the tension. "You're Mr. Hensley, aren't you?" she said to Old Rob. "Mrs. Hagstrom told me who you were." Her delicate, pretty hand reached for his. "I can't tell you how grateful I am."

Old Rob coughed. "I'm glad y' come," he said, and began to wipe his hand against one hip. Spike gave a low growl of disapproval, and he bent down to the dog. "Quiet!" he snapped with more than necessary force, and when he straightened he did not offer his hand.

Jane wanted to cry out: "You don't need to thank him for anything he's done, Alice. This isn't like any other house you've ever been in! These aren't real people at all!"

The old man must have been a little ashamed of his rudeness. "I guess Spike'll be quiet now," he muttered, with a glance at Alice over the bridge of his nose. "Y' want t' come in th' house?" Jane felt that it was not because he wanted them to, but because he almost had to. Old Rob doubtless wanted them to go away, as fast as possible.

"Yes. Yes," said the tall woman, "let's go in." She

glanced again toward the split elm. "Let's wait inside."

"If it's all right with you," the stout man said to Old Rob.

"You—y' ain't got long t' wait?" Old Rob countered, as though he had made a mistake.

"Oh, no. But the ladies are tuckered out. Be nice if they could sit down for a while." The stout man's face grew redder as he spoke.

"All right," Old Rob said thoughtfully. "All right. Come on in." He went to the screen door, held it open, and the small procession filed into the house.

Jane had a sensation that they all moved reluctantly, that they should not be going in there at all. She wanted to call out to Alice, "Come back. If you're tired, let's sit in the car, where we can talk in peace." But Alice and Mrs. Hagstrom and the men were all in the kitchen.

Before any of them were seated, Cokey had her mother's hand. "Oh, Moms," she pleaded, "why do we have to wait?"

"They're fixing the bridge. It won't take long."

"Oh," Cokey said, "the bridge."

Jane was looking at Alice with her brave smile, and she could see that Alice was tired. But above all, Alice was intensely grateful for having found them.

Jane and Cokey were back on the couch again, and Alice was seated between them. Jane had a vague picture of old Rob Hensley waving one hand toward the table. The three others walked across the room and found chairs. Jane heard the chairs scraping but she was not watching the others, she was looking at Alice.

"You didn't tell us how you got here," she marveled. "How did you ever find us?"

Alice gave a sigh. "It's a long story."

"I'll bet it is," Cokey said fervently. "Tell us!"

Cokey seemed to have forgotten her surroundings, to have thrown off the spell of the place. Alice looked at her fondly, her gaze drifting to the tousled hair and the bedraggled dress. A second look took in Jane's disheveled appearance, but she said nothing of that. "What about you two?" Alice asked. "You missed the way to Keegans', didn't you?"

Cokey was amazed. "Honestly, Moms, do you know everything?"

"Not quite, or I would have been here sooner."

"But—how?" Jane asked.

"You left a trail," Alice said wisely. "Remember the man you asked to tell you the way to the Baker Road?"

"Why, yes," Jane said slowly. "It was out in front of Martha Burke's house. Just after we left the woman—after promising to take her message for her."

"Well," Alice continued, "I found the Baker Road—" she looked over at the stout man and smiled, "but I'm ahead of myself. First of all, I found Mr. Hagstrom. He was on his way home."

"But—" Cokey said vaguely, "we had the car. Did you walk, Moms?"

"Some. I'm a good hiker."

She walked, Jane thought, hiked along to find us. And this was all my fault. I have to tell her that. I have to explain.

But there was no time for explanations now. Alice had too much to tell them.

"As I was saying," Alice took up her story, "Mr. Hagstrom took me to his home. He said you had probably passed his house. Almost everybody did."

"That's right," the ruddy-faced man added. "And they did, too."

But he was not at ease by any means. Jane glanced at him as he spoke, and she saw that the three had pulled their chairs close together. They looked anything but comfortable.

Alice smiled at him, and he nodded toward the tall woman. "It was Josie here, you talked to. Josie was worried after she let you go on through."

"Yes, I was." The manner in which the tall woman spoke, showed plainly that her worries were not at an end. "I got to thinking, I never should have let you girls try to get through to—" She paused to look at the lean man who had remained silent. "—to Bill Keegan's place."

Jane said to him, "Oh, are you Bill Keegan? We

"You Left a Trail," Alice Said Wisely

were going to bring you a message from your sister."

"I know," the man nodded kindly. "She told me. I was in there this morning." Stern lines appeared around his mouth. "She never should have let you go."

"She was hurt," Jane protested, "and she was worried. It was my fault for telling her we would." Now was the time to tell Alice Champlin. Now she could take all the blame. "I didn't have any right to make such a promise," Jane spoke, "when you were expecting us—and it was going to storm. It was all my fault this terrible thing happened."

Even before she realized that she had said it, the words were out—*this terrible thing.*

Alice Champlin shook her head, refusing to let Jane assume such a weight of responsibility, but the reaction of the other three was something different. Old Rob Hensley stiffened in the rocking chair, but he was not rocking. Jane saw him biting his lower lip and rubbing his hands together nervously.

Josie Hagstrom leaned forward in her chair. "What happened?" she said. "Something terrible, you say?"

The stout man put a hand on her arm. "Now, Josie," he said.

She brushed him off. "I got to know, Fred."

Bill Keegan laughed on a high key. "*They're* all right," he pointed out. "Everything turned out all right. And we'll be leaving soon." He stood up.

"Maybe, if you're rested, we'd better leave right away."

"I don't like it on the outside of the place," Josie Hagstrom said. She looked at Alice. "Not unless you don't mind keeping right on going till we get back to the bridge?"

Alice Champlin knew that there were currents underneath their thoughts that she could not fathom. She must have sensed something of the sinister atmosphere around the Frieson place. Jane knew, however, that these people had not told her the story of Simmering Springs and the Swamp Wizard. Probably they had not wanted to worry Alice, to cause her unnecessary pain. Jane's thoughts flew back to the moment when they had first approached the house. She remembered now that none of the three had been at ease, but they had been deeply, tremendously relieved because the girls were safe. They had been afraid that something might have happened to them. They had come in, only because they wanted Alice to rest. Now, they wanted to leave as soon as possible.

That was the way it seemed. Perhaps Jane was wrong, but there was no mistaking the intensity of feeling in Josie Hagstrom's face. "You didn't—hear anything out of the ordinary, did you?"

She was asking that of Jane, and the girl's throat suddenly tightened. Did they hear anything out of the ordinary?

Indeed they had! A horrible scream that cut through the night—the cry of the Swamp Wizard— a cry that came because strange feet had been set on Frieson land.

Strange feet, Jane thought. The others must know that story. They are afraid. They have not been here for months—perhaps for years. And they would not be here now if it had not been to show Alice Champlin the way. Yes, that was it. Josie Hagstrom said, "We had to come to find out if you were here. We figured when you didn't come to the Keegans', you missed your way. But we don't have to stay here!" She stood up, her eyes fixed on the ruddy-faced man. "We don't have to stay here!" she repeated. "I can tell by the look on that girl's face— by the look on both of them—that they. . . ."

Old Rob came to his feet and the rocking chair continued to sway behind him, "No, y' don't have t' stay," he agreed angrily. "Y' came here an' y' found 'em, an' now y' can git out. Any time y' want t' go, I hain't stoppin' ya'!"

They were all looking at him, and during that minute—or maybe only a second, Jane did not know—it was quiet enough to hear the creak of the door to Alma Frieson's room. All heads turned toward the sound and everyone waited in deathly silence. Presently the woman came in, her face the rigid mask Jane knew so well. Slowly, carefully, the dark eyes appraised the people in the room. Her attention did not dwell upon Alice and the two girls for long, but came back to the three new arrivals near the table. Josie Hagstrom and her husband were still standing, and Bill Keegan came to his feet. It was Josie who spoke.

"Why, hello, Alma. You're looking—well." She was painfully ill at ease, and she looked it. But Alma Frieson maintained a deadly quiet. Only the corner of her mouth twitched. She said, flatly, "Am I?" Then she faced her father. "You should have come in and told me I had company." Again the lips twisted. "If I hadn't waked up, I might not have known it."

The old man began to splutter some explanation, but Josie Hagstrom made another valiant attempt to be a good neighbor. "Oh, were you napping? I'm so sorry we disturbed you."

Alma Frieson's eyes were like cubes of ice. "I fell on the cellar steps," she said. "I hurt myself, or I wouldn't be in bed, not at this time of day. You can report that, too, when you get back."

"Why—I—" Josie Hagstrom seemed close to tears.

"And you," Alma Frieson said as she turned to Bill Keegan, "you can tell your sister-in-law the same thing. Why I wasn't here, ready for company. And you might tell Martha that my house was clean, even though a couple of busybodies have been poking around in it for the last twenty-four hours."

Alice must have known she meant the girls, and gave a gasp of astonishment. Jane saw Alice's eyes, wide and puzzled, trained on the grim figure as it moved nearer the stove.

"Martha knows your house is clean," Bill Keegan said. "It always was."

The gaunt woman sniffed. "Does she? I don't think so. It's—a number of years since Martha has been out here."

"Well, that's not Martha's fault," Bill Keegan said heatedly. "You just about told her to stay away, as I remember it. You haven't been exactly sociable yourself, Alma!"

The ruddy-faced man coughed uneasily. His wife had whispered something to him and he nodded, saying almost at the same time, "I think we better go. The bridge'll be ready by now." He looked over toward Alice. She was standing, Jane realized, and the girls both stood up. "This little lady was mighty worried about her girls," the man continued. "We only stopped so she could get her breath. I guess the bridge is fixed by now. Or it will be soon. They're working on it."

Alice was out of her depth, but in this murky place she was as brilliant as the jewel that she really was. She walked toward Alma Frieson and smiled into the set face. "I'm so grateful to you for letting the girls stay here. I hope they haven't been too much trouble. I hope sometime you'll come and

visit us.''

Alice would never know how strange that sounded—hoping that Alma Frieson would come sometime and visit at the brown house under the apple trees! She belonged *here,* in a house beside a split elm, near the spitefully boiling spring, and the swamp that hemmed them in from everything kind and beautiful.

Jane wondered what the woman would say. It seemed they all wondered as they waited for Alma Frieson to speak. Jane felt that the whole house was waiting.

But the dark woman completely ignored the invitation. A frown cut into her forehead. She looked away from Alice, to the ruddy man. "You say the bridge is almost fixed by now? How long have they been working on it?"

"Since noon," he told her.

"Since—noon," Alma Frieson repeated slowly.

They could not know what was in her mind, but Jane knew and Cokey knew. It was since noon that Lem Frieson had come in and told them that the river was impassable and that there was no hope of returning that way. Why had he said that? Did he know the truth?

To cover the gap, the ruddy man went on: "We came over in a boat." His attempt to make it humorous failed utterly. "But you can drive the car back, Mrs. Champlin. Maybe we better get started now."

Alice nodded. "Yes, maybe we should."

"Yes, right away," urged Josie Hagstrom. She had her husband's arm and was urging him to move toward the door. "It'll be getting dark before we know it. And there's work to be done at home."

Alma Frieson seemed to emerge from the daze that engulfed her. "Yes, go," she said, moving back toward Rob Hensley who stood near the cupboard. "Go, all of you. Nobody comes to this house any more. Nobody—"

She broke off abruptly, for above her rising voice, came the cry that Jane had heard before—the piercing, hateful cry. Cokey had heard it, too, and her hand went up over her mouth. One of the men muttered sharply. Someone pushed a chair. It was Josie Hagstrom who cried out in abject terror— "The Swamp Wizard!"

CHAPTER ELEVEN

TRAPPED IN FEAR

There was utter confusion in the kitchen of the Frieson home. The tumult had long been raging in the minds of the Hagstroms and Bill Keegan, but the iron reserve of Alma Frieson held them in a shell of terror. Now it was the gaunt Frieson woman who broke under the spell of the hateful cry. Ashen-faced, she darted for the door, paused to wring her hands, and confronted her father who cringed back against the closed doors of the cupboard.

"Lem's out there!" Her voice rang above the muttering of the men and Josie Hagstrom's terrified whimpering. "Do you understand it? Lem's out there!"

"I know it!" The white head nodded. "I know he is!"

Her hands went up. "If anything happened to Lem—" She broke off, a hand went around the room, including the whole group. "Why did you let them come in here? Were you out of your mind?!"

"They said it was only for a spell," old Rob Hensley protested. "They come t' take the girls

215

away. I thought it was good riddance."

"Good riddance!" The echo came shrilly. "If anything happens to Lem!" With an effort, she controlled her voice. She sent a withering look at Josie Hagstrom. "What have you got to cry about? No boy of yours is out there!"

"I—I know—but—" the woman faltered.

"You're safe enough in here," Alma Frieson continued bitterly. "You—and all the rest!" Her eyes were beady black. "You can go back now to the village. Tell them the place is haunted. Tell everybody this is a haunted house!"

Alice Champlin drew a quick, deep breath. Jane looked at her, and Cokey crushed close to her side. Alice was trying to comprehend some of the meaning of the distorted scene. She looked from Cokey to Jane in strained puzzlement. "Do you know what they're talking about?" she asked of Jane.

"Some of it," Jane responded. "We can't explain —here. That's why we want to go."

Jane had spoken low, but Alma Frieson heard. "Yes, you want to go! I wish you had never come here! A mistake! That's what you said, a mistake! It's some secret plan, all of you are in it! You are spying on us! Bringing trouble on us!"

Bill Keegan burst out: "Now, Alma, that's not true. You know that's not true!"

"I know you haven't set foot on this place in years, Bill Keegan. No one from the hollow, nor the village. Why do you come here now? I tell you, if anything's happened to Lem—"

And then Jane remembered that this woman had suffered an injury not so many hours ago. She had been in bed most of the afternoon, and would never have remained there, if she had not been in pain. Alma Frieson had never admitted so wildly her fear before. Now Jane knew that the woman was terrified at the cry that rose from the swamp. Alma Frieson admitted by her actions that she believed the fearful legend of the Swamp Wizard.

"I'm sure nothing's happened to Lem," Jane said staunchly. "He was all right the other evening, when the—when the cry came."

"He was safe in his bed," Alma Frieson pointed out. "Of course he was safe then."

"Not the first time," Jane insisted. "He was out in the machine shed and you went and brought him in. Do you remember?"

The woman shook her head irritably. "How do you know? How can you tell?"

"Well, it's true, isn't it? Nothing would happen to Lem, I'm sure of it. He—he belongs here."

The gaunt woman seemed to wilt slowly. Her shoulders drooped, her unwieldly hands sagged at her side. Jane went nearer to her, motioning to old Rob Hensley. "Your daughter should go back to her room. There's nothing for her to worry about. Tell her so."

Old Rob did not believe Jane. His fears were far graver than Alma Frieson's. Jane tried to override them. "Tell her!" she insisted. "She's not able to stand here!"

"Come and lie down, girl," Old Rob said, and it was with an effort. "Lem—Lem's all right."

"How do you know?" The woman said listlessly. "How do you know?" They managed to lead her from the room. At her door, Jane said: "You help her in. Call us if you need us."

The old man shot her a barbed glance. "We don't need you. All we need is t' have you get out. Th' quicker, the better."

Alma Frieson moaned softly, and her father disappeared into the room with her. Alice came to Jane's side. "She was hurt you said, Jane? Maybe we ought to go right on in? The woman seems dreadfully ill to me."

"I—I don't know," Jane said, bewildered. "But, it isn't like—like any ordinary house here, Alice."

"I'll say it isn't!" Cokey put in. "You can't imagine, Moms—"

"I can imagine a little. Don't you think we ought to be there with her?"

"Let's wait a while and see," Cokey urged. "Maybe it'd be better to get him to take care of her. She —she thinks we poke around."

Alice nodded. "So I understood. The poor woman," she sighed.

Josie Hagstrom was sitting in her chair, her hands over her face. Nearby stood her husband, arms folded. He would glance down at her, then at Bill Keegan who stood soberly beside him.

As Jane drew nearer, Bill Keegan said: "Josie won't go outside. She won't leave the house."

"Sure, she will," the stout man protested, patting the bent shoulder. But he was far from convincing. It was evident that he, too, was afraid to venture out of doors.

Josie Hagstrom lifted her head. "No, I won't go out, Fred!" she said stubbornly. "Maybe—maybe nothing will happen to Lem, because he belongs here. But we don't! Can't you see? We don't belong here!"

Jane looked at Alice, even as Cokey was looking at her. Alice would know what to do. She always knew what to do. Why, she even found them here!

"The car is just outside the door," Alice said, thoughtfully. "We could hurry out and drive over to the river anyhow, and wait until—"

Josie Hagstrom's eyes were wide with horror. "We'd never get there," she said hoarsely. "We'd never live to see the river!"

"Now, Josie—" the stout man protested feebly.

"You know it's the truth. You heard that—that screech. That's the Swamp Wizard!"

Bill Keegan offered, "But if we hurried, like Mrs. Champlin said—"

"No!" Josie cried. "I tell you I won't go. Not until Lem comes back. I know Lem better than I do his mother. We went to school together. When Lem comes back, I'll ask him."

And then her husband said the unfortunate thing that clearly demonstrated his own fear: "But what if Lem doesn't come back?"

"If he doesn't come back!" Josie Hagstrom cried out. "Well, then you'll know for sure." She struggled to gain composure. "But he will. It won't hurt him. It—it can't hurt him."

"I—I guess not," Bill Keegan said hesitantly.

Josie Hagstrom's head came up. "You're thinking of—her, isn't that right? That maybe it wasn't a train wreck?"

"Keep quiet, Josie," Fred Hagstrom said gruffly. "You don't know what you're talking about!"

"Maybe I don't," the woman admitted shortly. "Maybe there's nothing queer about this place. Maybe everybody's been imagining it all these years." She looked from Jane to Cokey, who stood beside Alice. "But you girls were here all last night, weren't you? Maybe you know something more you can tell us." She was standing now, her hands writhing together. "I knew when I looked at you that you'd been through a siege of something or other."

A siege, Jane thought. Yes, it had been something of a siege. But when Alice and these people had appeared it had seemed the siege was over and

"I Won't Go," Josie Cried, "Till Lem Comes Back."

the road away from the Frieson farm was clear again.

However, the way was not clear. They were still trapped in fear, and now they had, as fellow prisoners, Alice and these three who had known the Friesons for years.

Cokey answered the woman: "We heard that same cry last night."

"Twice," Josie Hagstrom said with a kind of wild triumph. "They heard it twice! And I bet you Alma Frieson told you it was because you were a stranger, didn't she?"

Jane and Cokey exchanged a quick glance. Both the girls were in a maze, striving to cope with this new drawback to their release from the Frieson house. "No, I think it was Rob Hensley who told us about that," Jane said. "Anyway, he did down at the Pool."

This drew a sharp breath from Fred Hagstrom. "You mean—he took you down there? Past the picnic grounds?"

"He practically forced us to go there," Cokey said, "with that beastly dog of his."

"Cokey," Alice asked, "what is this pool? Where is it?"

"Down past the barn. It's a spring, Moms. They call it Simmering Springs. It kind of boils and bubbles all the time."

Josie Hagstrom gave a low moan. "It's all quick-

sand. No one ever dares to go near it. Not any
more."

"Why not any more?" Alice asked.

"I don't know," Josie went on dolefully. "It hasn't
always been that way. There was the picnic
ground—"

"It's no picnic ground now," Jane said ruefully.
"All weeds and the benches are a wreck."

"But it used to be," Bill Keegan insisted. "We
used to have fun down there in the old days."

Alice was growing impatient, and Jane knew that
she was. "You didn't tell me why nobody could go
near the pool any more," Alice addressed Josie.

"It's because of the Swamp Wizard." Her voice
was low, weighted with fear. "If a strange foot is
set near there, you hear the cry!"

"But none of us was near the pool," Alice argued.
"And still we heard that cry—as you call it."

"I know." Fred Hagstrom sounded impatient, as
though he wished they might talk about something
else. "But it's a good place to keep away from, let
me tell you that."

Alice looked from Jane to Cokey. "And you were
down there. I wonder why?"

Jane stared at Cokey knowingly, as if to instruct
her not to mention that they suspected the old man
of attempting to push them into the quicksands. "I
think Rob Hensley wanted to make sure we'd never
come back," she said loudly, hastily, "or bring any-

body else here. He wanted to scare the living day-lights out of us."

"And he succeeded," Cokey added. "We're ready to leave any time."

Josie Hagstrom was standing, and she approached Cokey. "Not now!" she pleaded. "We can't go now! You were around here long enough, so you ought to know it isn't safe."

"But," Cokey argued, "it'll be getting dark—"

"Please!" The big woman said piteously. "Please, wait till Lem gets here. He'll know what's best."

Would he? Jane wondered suddenly. While they had begun to believe that he was showing consider-ation for them, even worrying over their safety, the bridge had been undergoing repairs. Lem must have known that. He had left in that direction, and he was near enough to see that the work was being done. Yet he had led them to believe they had no hope of escape. He had said they should stay on here until the way was clear. He even went so far as to promise that no harm would come to them!

"Lem wanted us to go," Jane said suddenly, "they all did. But Lem said we couldn't get away."

Alice put a hand impulsively around each girlish shoulder. "You poor chickens," she said, not too comfortingly, or they might have given in then and there to the long, wearying strain. "You've been through a tight situation."

"If you ask me," Josie Hagstrom moaned, "they're

not through it yet. None of us are through it yet.
We might be here all night!"

"I hope not," Fred Hagstrom blurted. "I got
work waiting for me."

Bill Keegan said, inelegantly: "Me, too." He
shrugged his shoulders. "But Lem'll be coming
soon."

The sound of a door opening caused all eyes to
turn toward the entrance near the washstand—
Alma Frieson's door. Old Rob Hensley was returning, and as he left the room he methodically closed
the door as he had done before. If I have to see
that old man shutting that door one more time,
Jane thought wildly, I'll open my mouth and
scream. But she remained still, as did all the others,
watching the thin figure move across the floor.

He paused near the rocker and looked toward
them, but evaded a direct approach. "She's restin'.
That was a bad fall she had."

"If there's anything we can do," Alice said,
"please say so. We plan to leave the moment Lem
gets back." She nodded toward the tall woman.
"Mrs. Hagstrom feels she would rather wait until
he does."

The old man grunted. "Wait if y' want to. Mebbe
he won't come back."

"Oh, he will," Cokey said. "He always did
before."

"There's always a first time," the old man said

darkly, and seemed to enjoy the silence that hung over their heads. He gave a loud sigh and looked toward the clock. "It's after six. I'm goin' t' have some supper. Josie, if y' want to, you can set th' table for yourselves."

It was by no means a cordial invitation, but Jane welcomed it none the less and the group seemed to brighten visibly.

"Jane and I are starved," Cokey said under her breath.

Josie lost some of her gloom in taking charge as she had been told. With Alice and the girls assisting, the fresh bread, butter, cold meat and sauce were placed upon the table. Old Rob looked it over. "I guess that's enough," he said, and was the first to seat himself.

"Maybe," Jane whispered to Cokey, "there's a grumpier, meaner old man someplace but I don't know where."

The sound of scraping silverware and the chink of a cup as it was placed on a saucer broke an otherwise quiet, grim meal. They all waited tensely for the sound of the shed door as it opened, and they all feared the sound of another dismal cry.

But it did not come.

Water was heated on the stove and the women washed the dishes while the men remained in glum silence at the table. Alice had asked if she might not take a tray in to Alma Frieson, but Old Rob said to let her alone, that he would fix something for her later.

When the last cup was hung on its curved hook in the cupboard and the towels were folded and hung neatly by the stove, Alice announced: "I'm going in there, Mr. Hensley. I'll just take her a bite. If she doesn't want it, I'll bring it out again."

"All she wants is for Lem t' come," Old Rob growled, "an' for you t' git out."

"That's exactly what we want too." Alice smiled sweetly, and went about getting the tray ready. Jane watched her with a glow of appreciation. She and Cokey were on the couch. "Mothers are handy things to have in a pinch," she whispered.

"Pinch is right!" Cokey agreed. "If Lem doesn't come pretty soon, Jane, I'm asking Moms to leave, and the rest can stay if they want to."

"Shush!" Jane cautioned.

Now that Josie Hagstrom had nothing more to occupy her hands, she looked ready to break down completely. To tell her that they would leave without her would be a catastrophe.

Alice went in with the tray as she wished, and the girls waited for Alma Frieson's voice to order Alice from the room. But minutes passed and there came only the murmur of Alice's voice in subdued tones. At length Cokey's mother returned. She looked as though she had won a small victory—the tray was empty.

But it was growing dark now and the work on the bridge must have been completed. Jane shared Cokey's determination to leave the Frieson place. She admitted to herself that the Hagstroms and Bill Keegan had done a remarkably kind thing to bring Alice here in spite of their fear of the place, but still it might be the best thing to force them away. Jane recalled with a shudder how that eerie cry had pierced the night. Josie Hagstrom would surely go to pieces if it occurred again.

When darkness had really settled, old man Hensley, with a kind of ceremonial gesture, lighted the lamp and put it in its wall socket. It was then that the cry came the second time that night. They had been expecting it, of course, but still they were all horribly surprised. All experienced the same shock, but they reacted differently. Bill Keegan announced that he was leaving the place—that he had heard all he wanted to hear. Josie Hagstrom pleaded with him to wait half an hour longer to see if Lem would return. Her husband's fat cheeks looked drained and saggy in the lamplight. Alice said little, but placed her arms closer about each of the girls. She was thinking of last night, Jane knew, when the two girls were here alone with the Friesons.

Having Alice with them was a solace, of course, but it deepened Jane's sense of guilt. Now Alice was in this thing, too. She had been telling herself for some time that this was all her fault.

When Alma Frieson walked back into the kitchen, she was more like herself again—grim, unrelenting. "You heard that," she said to the group. "Now, if Lem isn't back here in less than twenty minutes, I'm going out to look for him." She looked at Bill Keegan and Fred Hagstrom. "You can go with me or not as you choose."

She was daring them to go—and giving them twenty minutes to think it over. Jane wondered about that. The night before Alma Frieson had brushed away her father's protests and had gone out immediately into the storm. She had found Lem and she had brought him back. She's hesitating now, Jane thought, because she's still weak. She's not sure of herself. She's hoping Lem will come in before then.

But whatever Alma Frieson planned to do about going out to look for her son, it was not necessary. The scraping of the outer screen door was heard, followed by steps in the shed. The gaunt woman's eyes seemed to come alive. "Lem!" she cried, and threw the kitchen door wide open.

Lem was caked with clay, and he looked as though he had labored at a back-breaking task for hours. "It's not quite—" he said to his mother and then his eyes rested on the newcomers. "I thought you went away," he said startled. "I thought I heard your car!"

"All you heard was the Swamp Wizard!" Josie

Hagstrom exploded. "Now, you tell us, Lem, if it's safe to leave here!"

"Safe?" The man pulled his cap off and ran a hand through his hair. "I don't know about the bridge," he began hesitantly, as he handed the cap to Alma Frieson.

"Oh, that's about fixed," Bill Keegan said. "Josie means—that screech. She's worried for fear we'll be bothered if we go."

"I'm worried!" Josie Hagstrom flared. "I guess you are, too, Bill Keegan. I'm not the only one." She walked over toward Lem. "Now, Lem, you tell us the truth."

Lem looked at his mother. "Didn't you tell them they could go?"

"No, how could I know?" Her voice broke. "Oh, Lem, you had me so worried."

"I was working on the road." He looked at her quickly. "You feeling better?"

"I'm all right," she said, and it seemed that she was now that Lem was safely back. Her shoulders squared and she said to Josie Hagstrom: "I don't see any reason why you can't go—the sooner, the better."

The big woman shook her head stubbornly. "I'd rather have Lem tell me!"

But what Lem might have told her went forever unsaid. They all heard the soft sound of the motor and saw the stream of light coming in through the window near the stove. Alma Frieson was directly in its glare and she threw one hand up over her eyes as if to ward off a physical blow.

"Now what under th' sun," Old Rob exploded. "First y' worry your mother half to death—an' now this comes! See what it is, Lem!"

The younger man was still near the door. He looked at it anxiously for a moment, and then went out. Alma Frieson called: "I'll hold the kitchen door open."

Jane heard the newcomer's voice before she saw him. "Who is that?" she thought. "That voice is terribly familiar!" And then he entered—a boy, thin and straight, with a mop of shaggy yellow hair and a bright grin.

"Eddie!" Alice and Cokey cried out in one voice, and Jane added: "Why, Eddie Champlin!"

"Well, I'll be—" The boy's eyes widened at the sight of the three of them. "What in the heck is going on here? What are you doing here?"

"And what are *you* doing here?" Alice Champlin asked.

"And where's the tractor?" Cokey added.

"Out in the yard." He pointed to the glaring lights in the window. "It took longer than I thought to get the thing. Nice isn't it? And quiet as a mouse."

"It's simply beautiful!" Cokey said with some return of her old sparkle. "I see in the dark like a cat."

"Have you seen yourself lately?" Eddie inquired. He gave Jane a quick look. "You look swell, Jane."

"That's malarkey," Jane responded. She felt better, too, since Eddie had arrived. Indeed, he seemed to command the Frieson kitchen now. Everyone in the little group was watching him.

"But she's swell," Eddie said to his mother, and grinned. "The tractor, I mean. Muffler, rubber tires—only the lights go on the blink now and then." He turned to look at Lem. "I was sure grateful for that lantern of yours down in the swamp hole, mister," he said warmly. "I could see you there plain as day. Was I ever stalled!"

There was a silence in the room like the calm before a storm. Although it did not break, Eddie, too, was aware of the gathering clouds. His grin was as broad as ever, but a quizzical light gleamed in his blue-green eyes. "But you got to show me that trick whistle of yours, mister. Say, that beats anything I ever heard!"

Eddie was on the outside looking in on a drama he could not understand. He had not seen the prologue or the first two acts, and this was the climax —a climax which was too piercingly sharp and intense for Alma Frieson to endure. It was she who broke the silence by falling to the floor in a dead faint.

CHAPTER TWELVE

HOUSEWARMING

Lem was kneeling on the floor, close to the couch. Alma Frieson was lying there, her head on the pillow Alice had asked Jane to bring from her room. Cokey had brought the light quilt to cover her. Alma Frieson's eyes were open now, not bright and beady-black, but puzzled with a hurt too deep for words. She saw no one in the big kitchen except Lem. And she also seemed unaware of Old Rob over near the washstand, and the three neighbors huddled in awed silence beside the table. Nor did she appear to notice Alice, Eddie, and the two girls standing back of him a little way off.

Lem was saying, brokenly, once again, "You can understand it, mother. I can make you understand it."

Jane had never heard him call her "mother" before. Somehow the picture tore at her heart—the man kneeling there with mud-caked boots, his black tousled hair straggling over his forehead, rubbing his mother's listless hand—was enough to fill anyone with pity.

Was Lem Frieson the voice of the Swamp Wizard? That was what Alma Frieson was asking herself

as Lem assured her that he could explain everything so that she would understand. It was not easy
for Fred and Josie Hagstrom and Bill Keegan to
understand. They had lived in a totally different
manner for many years. As for old Rob Hensley,
whose faith in the evil power had been unshakable,
his face was a mask with eyes staring at Lem as
though he were a spirit from another world.

Alma Frieson's lips moved with an effort. "Why,
Lem," she said, "why did you do it?"

Jane saw something bright on his cheek. He
reached up to brush it away.

"To keep them away. That was all."

The woman moistened her lips. Her eyes were
straight on her son's face. When she spoke, it was
with a tremendous effort. "It was—the way—Rob
thought?"

Lem nodded. "Yes. It was that way."

Alma Frieson turned her head to the wall—away
from everything. Lem tried to draw her back.

"It was an accident, mother. You've got to believe
that! It was an accident!"

Her head tried to nod, but her face avoided his.

"In Heaven's name, mother, say that you believe
me!"

Her hand found his, then slowly, she turned
toward him again. "Yes, Lem. I believe you. But
I wish—I wish you had told me the truth. I have
blamed myself—all these years."

"Why Did You Do It, Lem?" Alma Frieson Asked

"Blamed yourself! How could you?"

"I thought I shouldn't have let her go on that trip. She was such a little girl."

"She wasn't so little. Even if she had gone, that still wouldn't have been your fault. It—it wasn't anybody's fault."

Alma Frieson's eyes closed, but she clasped her hand tightly in that of her son. Near the stove, old Rob Hensley made a sound like a sob, and Eddie whispered to Jane, who stood nearest to him: "What's going on here, anyway? Did I do all this?"

"You didn't do any of it, Eddie—except clear up some kind of a dreadful mistake," Jane said softly. "I don't know what it is, exactly, but I'm sure it's all for the best. You wait and see."

The conversation, though it could hardly have been overheard, brought the group of friendly neighbors to their side. Josie Hagstrom said, in what she believed to be a quiet tone: "Don't you think we better go now? This is a family affair, and not for our ears."

Lem Frieson heard her. Still on his knees, he turned, and came to his feet. He looked taller, younger, as he had seemed when he was running toward the house from the pool on the previous day.

"No, Josie," he spoke purposefully, "I want you to stay. You're in on this much of it, you might as well stay for the finish." He nodded toward the two men. "You, too, Bill and Fred, you stay."

Alice was quick to observe that he had not included Jane and the Champlins. She smiled at Lem. "We'll wait out in the car."

"Oh, no." He shook his head. "You wait here, too," he said, and added as an afterthought: "If you please."

"Why—certainly," Alice said. "If we're not intruding."

"I owe it to the girls—to all of you. I'm going to tell the whole story, as soon as my mother can sit up."

Alma Frieson raised herself on one elbow. "Tell it now, Lem," she said, and glanced about at the intense row of faces. "You're sure you want—them?"

"I'm sure." His voice was deep, true. He looked over at his grandfather. "Rob, I wish you'd sit down in that rocker."

"Me sit down?" It was a feeble protest, and Jane could see one of his hands shaking. "Oh, all right, all right." Muttering under his breath, he obeyed.

Jane found the extra pillows and Alice tucked them back of Alma Frieson. Her face was still very pale, but quiet and peaceful as though she were enduring great pain, but with a certain amount of relief. She moved closer to the wall and motioned to a place at her side. "Sit here, Lem, where I can hold your hand."

It was in this manner that Lem began his strange story.

"I had a sister, Evie, six years younger than myself," he began. "We were always the greatest of pals, Evie and I."

Jane saw Alma Frieson's other hand move instinctively to the black cameo locket, and she knew at once that the picture inside it was of Evie.

There was a momentary pause in which Jane heard Josie Hagstrom's quick intake of breath. Lem looked over at her. "You remember Evie?"

The men nodded and Josie said, eagerly, "Oh, yes! Sure I do!"

Lem sought the right word and found it. "We—Evie and I—knew all the Indian stories about Simmering Springs. I don't think we really believed any of them, about the curse that came when a strange foot would be set on the place, but it was kind of spooky, and fun, to pretend that we believed in the Swamp Wizard." He looked over at Old Rob, a graven image in the rocker. "I think you always believed in it, though, Rob."

The old man made no answer. He simply looked at the younger man, waiting for him to unfold the story. Lem stroked his mother's hand again and Jane was grateful to see that her fingers were returning some of his affection. "I'll make this as short as I can," Lem continued. "My mother's been hurt and you people want to go home. You can go now. The bridge is fixed."

"It is?" Bill Keegan blurted happily.

"Yes. I saw it was, just before I—before I went back over to the swamp."

"Yes, Lem?" Alma Frieson said. "Tell me—about that night."

"Evie wanted to go to the city to visit our cousins. She was sixteen then, but she was always little for her age. Mother"—he looked at her lovingly, "mother thought she was too young."

Alma Frieson closed her eyes, nodded, and opened them again.

"I was supposed to take Evie over to the junction that night, because it saved time. That train was wrecked at the high bridge. They didn't find half of—the bodies." He glanced swiftly into his mother's face as much as to say, "Is it all right?"

Her head nodded approval and Lem took a deep breath. "I let my mother—and everybody else— think that Evie was on that train. But she wasn't. We never got to the junction. Evie—Evie went down in—the pool."

It was then a sob was wrenched from Alma Frieson's heart. There were other muted sobs in the room. Josie Hagstrom cried out softly, and Jane thought Old Rob did too.

"We went down to say good night to the Wizard," Lem continued. "It was a silly thing to do, but Evie always got a kick out of pretending. Besides, I don't think she really wanted to take that train. She was always a great one to stick at home."

He did not look at his mother, but over her head, into another tragic time. "I don't know myself, I can't say just how it happened she slipped and fell. At first I was too—too surprised to know it. She was running one minute, and falling the next. I grabbed for her, and she tried to reach my hand. But—she went down. She—went—down."

His head bent and no sound came from his lips. His shoulders moved with a terrific effort to hide the depth of his emotion. Alma Frieson patted his hands with loving understanding. "It's all right, Lem," she begged him to believe her. "It's—all right, son. Just knowing for sure—it's such a load off my heart!"

The room was silent as everyone waited for Lem to continue, but he could not find the words.

"Tell me this, Lem," Alma Frieson said, hesitatingly, "what did she say? Did she—say anything?"

"Just called out my name. She just called, 'Lem.' It went quick, mother. Faster than you'd think."

Again, the dark head on the pillows turned to the wall. The clock on the shelf could be heard ticking as if keeping time with Alma Frieson's heart and ticking out her grief. Time turned back again to the beginning of the terror that had gripped the Frieson farm. In his explanation of the terror, Jane remembered what Lem had said: "To keep them away." That was the purpose he had had in mind in maintaining the legend of the evil menace of the swamp and the springs.

But he was going to tell it to them, again, clearly.

"I knew that nothing that—that went down—ever came up," he went on resolutely. "At least, that was what everyone said. But I kept thinking, suppose Evie does come up. Suppose somebody thinks I pushed her in. Most of all," he looked directly into his mother's face, "most of all, I thought *you* might think that."

"I think—that—" Alma Frieson gasped. "Why Lem!"

"Well, Evie was so pretty. I always thought she was your favorite."

Mrs. Frieson sprang to an upright position. "Look at me, Lem," she commanded. "Look at me!

"I never had a favorite, Lem. I loved you both the same."

"And you don't hate me now?"

"Oh, Lem!" She drew a deep breath. "I only wish I had known before—for sure. I kept thinking that maybe she wasn't on that train, but you said you took her to the junction. And—after the wreck—"

"I know," the man cut in. "And all the while I wanted to tell you you'd never find her—there. She was in the pool."

Jane lifted her shoulders. They felt heavy, as though a great weight were pressing down upon her. Old Rob Hensley spoke with a sudden, crack-of-a-whip effect that put everyone on the alert.

"But how did y' manage it so slick?" he said. "I'd like t' know. Just what did y' do t' make that unearthly noise, scaring us half out of our wits?"

Lem was looking at Josie when he said: "I know a way to whistle through my fingers. I—I worked on that."

"Why, sure," Josie Hagstrom said, "you used to make the craziest imitations in school."

Old Rob, still confused, interrupted. "All th' time it was you, huh?" He was thinking back, trying to fathom how this was possible. "Yesterday evenin', after these girls came here, how did y' manage that?"

"I was out in the machine shed," Lem said.

"But th' cry—your whistle—it came from th' swamp!"

"You just thought it did."

Old Rob pondered that but suddenly interrupted: "Well, how about later on last night? When we looked in on y'. You were sleepin' then."

Lem shook his head. "No, I wasn't. You didn't go into my room, did you?"

"We looked in. Alma and me." He glanced to the woman for confirmation. But she was watching Lem, pity and love fighting for mastery in her gaze. "We saw you all rolled up in your bedding," Old Rob said, stubbornly.

"That's all you saw—the bedding," Lem sighed. "I didn't think you'd go way in. I had to take a chance on that." He looked toward Jane and Cokey for the first time. "I wanted you two to go away."

Jane found her voice. "And we certainly wanted to. But—but we couldn't have gone at that hour, could we?"

"No, you couldn't. I just wanted to make sure you'd go as soon as you could."

"But why did you want us to stay today?" Cokey asked. "You wouldn't let us try to swim—"

"I should say not. For one thing, it'd be too dangerous. And then, I was pretty sure they'd fix the bridge. I wanted you to wait till they did. So you could go in your car. I didn't want anybody else coming here." Now he looked at Bill Keegan, at Josie and Fred Hagstrom; at Alice and Eddie. "But it looks like plenty of you came anyhow."

"And I'm mighty glad we came!" Bill Keegan said with spirit. "It's about time this foolishness got settled once and for all. You should have told the truth, Lem. There's nobody in the world would ever believe you'd hurt a hair of Evie's head!"

Alma Frieson's eyes went to him warmly and she said: "You see, son?"

"I see, now. I—I must have been—crazy. But I got that idea of the Swamp Wizard worked up, and I couldn't seem to get rid of it. I—I—think I did the most wrong, mother."

"Oh, now that's not true!"

"Not only that, but making you break off with

all your friends. Scaring people away. You used to have so many friends."

Josie Hagstrom stepped forward. "I'd say she still has. I always liked you, Alma, no matter—" Jane knew she almost said: "No matter how mean you were!"

Alma Frieson then did a surprising thing. She smiled, and it was truly remarkable what it did for her. "No matter how ornery I was!" she said.

"You really believed in the Swamp Wizard, didn't you, Rob?" Fred Hagstrom asked as if to change the subject deliberately.

"Well—yes 'n no," the old man replied. "I thought it was a good idea to keep folks away, especially when it seemed t' make that whistle of Lem's."

But *he* didn't know that it was Lem's whistle, Jane thought, and *he did* believe in the Swamp Wizard! It was he who fostered the belief. Jane would not soon forget their visit to the Mystery Pool, with Spike trailing at their heels, and she wanted to hear the old man say for certain that he would never push anyone into the quicksand. That seemed terribly important.

"You wouldn't want to see anyone fall in there, would you?" Jane asked him, and for a minute she thought that he was going to shout back an answer.

"No." Old Rob Hensley shook his head. "I wouldn't let anyone fall in that pool. When I thought that young lady—" he pointed awkwardly to Cokey, "was goin' to slip in, I nearly had a conniption fit."

Eddie spoke up, sudden as a thunderclap. "Did Cokey fall in?"

"Would I be here?" Cokey asked him. "No, I slipped. That was all."

But old Rob had not finished. "Th' truth was I didn't want anyone around that spring. An' I wanted t' make sure y' girls would go an' never come back. Y' see—y' see." He coughed. "I had a kinda' hunch that maybe Evie didn't make t' train that night."

"You knew, Rob?" Lem asked.

"Oh, no. I just had a hunch. But I didn't want t' Swamp Wizard takin' anybody else. Not if I could help it."

Jane smiled at him. He had certainly given them the lesson the most difficult way—but it had been with a good enough intention. He had believed in the Swamp Wizard. He still believed in the Swamp Wizard! If something weren't done about it, he might go on believing and spreading the fantastic story that a spell hung over the Frieson farm.

But that was not going to be the case. Old Rob was by far outnumbered.

Alice Champlin came closer to the couch and said: "Mrs. Frieson, if there isn't anything more we can do, I think I'll take my brood home with me."

Alma Frieson showed her gratitude in another smile, and extended her hands. "You were good to me. And so were the girls." She glanced toward Cokey. "I'm sorry I was so sharp when you were at that door, but—that was—Evie's room."

Cokey nodded because she could not talk. Like Jane, she was filled with boundless gratitude. All of a sudden the clouds had lifted—there was no more mystery. The cry had been made by Lem Frieson! There was no Swamp Wizard!

"And thank you for all you did, my dear," Alma Frieson said to Jane. "You—you remind me of little —Evie."

"But—but," Jane stammered, "she was—beautiful."

"Always fishing for compliments," Eddie teased, "just like old times."

Jane simply grinned at him. She was too contented to do otherwise. And she was thinking what a blessing Cokey's kid brother and his balky tractor had been to them.

"Would you mind if we left the tractor here this evening?" Alice Champlin said smoothly. "We can come for it in the morning."

Eddie gave a start as though he had suffered a mortal wound, but Alice ignored him. Lem Frieson agreed to the proposal, and even Alma smiled her approval, and added that they would be expecting them.

They all said "Good night" moving toward the door. Suddenly Bill Keegan paused. "You know,"

"We're Going to Have a Lot of Fun This Summer."

he said slowly, "we were all here this evening, and we all know that Swamp Wizard story is a joke. We're spreading that around." He winked at Old Rob and directed: "Get your sickle out and get that grass cut in the picnic ground. We'll be using it."

There were more "Goodbyes" and more promises to come back soon before Alice Champlin had her brood gathered close and headed toward the car.

Eddie was grumbling. "I come in and save the day, and what happens? My tractor's taken away. That's gratitude for you!"

"Here's gratitude for you!" Alice Champlin hugged him and Eddie pretended deep disgust. He had a word of praise due him, and both Jane and Cokey would be quick to give it at the proper time and place.

Cokey was looking back to the lighted kitchen which now seemed warm and friendly. "That house looks as though it just had a housewarming," she laughed.

"It did," Jane added. In the dark Cokey could not see Jane's grin, but she must have known that her friend was about to burst into laughter.

"You know what, Cokey?" Jane snickered. "I've got a hunch!"

"A hunch?" Cokey choked.

"Yes," Jane continued, "I've a hunch we're going to have a lot of fun this summer!"

WHITMAN
AUTHORIZED EDITIONS

NEW STORIES OF ADVENTURE AND MYSTERY

Up-to-the-minute novels for boys and girls about Favorite Characters, all popular and well-known, including—

INVISIBLE SCARLET O'NEIL

LITTLE ORPHAN ANNIE and the Gila Monster Gang

BRENDA STARR, Girl Reporter

DICK TRACY, Ace Detective

TILLIE THE TOILER and the Masquerading Duchess

BLONDIE and Dagwood's Adventure in Magic

BLONDIE and Dagwood's Snapshot Clue

BLONDIE and Dagwood's Secret Service

JOHN PAYNE and the Menace at Hawk's Nest

BETTY GRABLE and the House With the Iron Shutters

BOOTS (of "Boots and Her Buddies") and the Mystery of the Unlucky Vase

ANN SHERIDAN and the Sign of the Sphinx

JANE WITHERS and the Swamp Wizard

WHITMAN
AUTHORIZED EDITIONS

JANE WITHERS and the Phantom Violin

JANE WITHERS and the Hidden Room

BONITA GRANVILLE and the Mystery of Star Island

ANN RUTHERFORD and the Key to Nightmare Hall

POLLY THE POWERS MODEL: The Puzzle of the Haunted Camera

JOYCE AND THE SECRET SQUADRON: A Captain Midnight Adventure

NINA AND SKEEZIX (of "Gasoline Alley"): The Problem of the Lost Ring

GINGER ROGERS and the Riddle of the Scarlet Cloak

SMILIN' JACK and the Daredevil Girl Pilot

APRIL KANE AND THE DRAGON LADY: A "Terry and the Pirates" Adventure

DEANNA DURBIN and the Adventure of Blue Valley

DEANNA DURBIN and the Feather of Flame

GENE AUTRY and the Thief River Outlaws

RED RYDER and the Mystery of the Whispering Walls

RED RYDER and the Secret of Wolf Canyon

The books listed above may be purchased at
the same store where you secured this book.

THE EXCITING NEW
FIGHTERS FOR FREEDOM SERIES

Thrilling novels of war and adventure for modern boys and girls

Kitty Carter of the CANTEEN CORPS

Nancy Dale, ARMY NURSE

March Anson and Scoot Bailey of the U.S. NAVY

Dick Donnelly of the PARATROOPS

Norma Kent of the WACS

Sally Scott of the WAVES

Barry Blake of the FLYING FORTRESS

Sparky Ames and Mary Mason of the FERRY COMMAND